D0824493

Armando Palacio Valdés

Bust of Armando Palacio Valdés on Calle de Palacio Valdés, Oviedo. Photo by Robert M. Fedorchek.

Armando Palacio Valdés

"Alone" and Other Stories

Translated from the Spanish by
Robert M. Fedorchek

Lewisburg
Bucknell University Press
London and Toronto: Associated University Presses

Associated University Presses
440 Forsgate Drive
Cranbury, NJ 08512

Associated University Presses
25 Sicilian Avenue
London WC1A 2QH, England

Associated University Presses
P.O. Box 338, Port Credit
Mississauga, Ontario,
L5G 4L8 Canada

The paper used in this publication meets the requirements
of the American National Standard for Permanence of Paper
for Printed Library Materials Z39.48-1984.

Library of Congress Cataloging-in-Publication Data

Palacio Valdés, Armando, 1853–1938.
   [Short stories. English. Selections]
   Armando Palacio Valdés : Alone, and other stories / translated
from the Spanish by Robert M. Fedorchek.
     p.   cm.
   Includes bibliographical references.
   ISBN 0-8387-5251-9 (alk. paper)
   1. Palacio Valdés, Armando, 1853–1938—Translations into English.
I. Fedorchek, Robert M., 1938–   . II. Title. III. Title: Alone, and
other stories.
PQ6629.A5A23   1993
863'.62—dc20   92-54400
                                                CIP

PRINTED IN THE UNITED STATES OF AMERICA

This translation is for my mother,
Mary Fedorchek,
whose compassion
is the definition of her life.

Contents

Translator's Foreword

The Asturian novelist and short story writer Armando Palacio Valdés was born during the reign of Isabel II and died in the waning years of the Second Republic, at the height of the Spanish Civil War. His contemporaries included such literary greats as Juan Valera, Benito Pérez Galdós, Emilia Pardo Bazán, and *Clarín* (Leopoldo Alas) from the nineteenth century, and Pío Baroja, Miguel de Unamuno, Ramón María del Valle-Inclán, and Antonio Machado from the twentieth. But although he witnessed the soul-searching and anguished questions asked by the Generation of 98, in outlook and form Palacio Valdés was and remained a quintessential nineteenth-century author who clung to a formula rooted solidly in Realism and Naturalism. Today, Valera, Galdós, Pardo Bazán, and *Clarín* are held in much higher regard as novelists than Palacio Valdés and have withstood better the test of time; on the other hand, he, along with Vicente Blasco Ibáñez, another of his contemporaries, was early on, unlike the above four, "discovered" in other countries and read in many foreign languages. Eleven of his novels were translated into English during his lifetime, and a number of them were also translated into French, German, Dutch, Italian, Czech, Portuguese, and Swedish, while the masterpieces of Galdós and *Clarín* have only recently been translated into English—the former's *Fortunata and Jacinta* in 1973 and 1986, and the latter's *La Regenta* in 1984.

If some of his novels are no longer held in high critical regard, many of Palacio Valdés's short stories will endure for their humor, irony, and understanding of human foibles. The late Spanish critic Mariano Baquero Goyanes considered him, along with Emilia Pardo Bazán and *Clarín*, one of nineteenth-century Spain's three best short story writers.

Like Cervantes, Palacio Valdés is fundamentally a humorist who looks upon man's shortcomings with avuncular forbearance. Many of his well-known Spanish contemporaries—Pedro Antonio de Alarcón, Juan Valera, Luis Coloma, Antonio Trueba, Jacinto Octavio Picón, José María Pereda, Benito Pérez Galdós—wrote the occasional story in which humor was the main element, but they never became known as humorous short story writers, with the exception of Alarcón, many of whose tales ("The Stub Book," and short novels, like *The Three Cornered Hat*), bubble with comic turns. In Palacio Valdés, however, it is a signature, a defining characteristic of his style as well as his indulgent commentary. There is—undeniably—humor in his fellow Asturian and friend *Clarín*, but it is a humor often laden with satire, some of it mordant like Swift's (and to a degree never reached by Palacio Valdés), which results in the satirist overshadowing the humorist. And Emilia Pardo Bazán, far and away the most prolific short story writer of the nineteenth or any other century, wrote nothing comparable to the mirth of "The Curate's Colt" or the drollery of "The Life of a Canon," or the merriment and fun poked by "Seduction" or the amusement triggered by the denouement of "The Crime on Perseguida Street."

A number of moving and powerful stories about children were written by nineteenth-century Spanish authors—Pérez Galdós's "The Mule and the Ox," *Clarín's* "Goodbye, Cordera!," Alarcón's "The Nun," Pardo Bazán's "First Love"—who demonstrated convincingly their ability to penetrate the spirit of the child who confronts pain and joy, i.e., the passage of life. Palacio Valdés's single most famous story, "Alone!," is about a three-year-old boy whose summer idyll changes from joy to pain, not completely cognizant of the tragedy that has befallen him. In *A Novelist's Life* [*La novela de un novelista*], an autobiographical tome dedicated, interestingly, to "Today's Children" (of 1921, when it was first published), Palacio Valdés recorded impressions of a summer spent in the country: "On hot days my father, Cayetano [the family's majordomo who had a dog named Muley, like the dog in "Polyphemus"], and I would go swimming in a river pool called Cuanya. It was located near a crag and shaded by an immense walnut tree. The biggest thrill of those swimming excursions was watching Cayetano dive into the water, stay under for several seconds, and always surface with a trout in his hand. So adept was he at finding them under stones that sometimes I saw him come up with two, one in each hand. But it would scare the life out of me. When it took him longer than usual I used to think that he had drowned and my heart would pound violently. Recollection of those anguished moments was the inspiration for my short story titled 'Alone!'" Palacio Valdés captures the child's desolation and despair so well that his felicitous treatment of a father's love is sometimes overlooked. The descriptions of Fresnedo with his son in the stable and the chicken coop, and their shared secrets in the straw loft, are the best of human touches, the purest of emotive exchanges—they are, quite simply, masterful renderings of timeless and universal feelings which underscore the poignancy and pathos of the ending.

Another splendid story about children, characteristically cloaked in a humorous style, is "Primitive Society," which captures the mettle of a Christian maiden—a seven-year-old girl who undergoes trial at the hands of a group of little boys in Madrid's Retiro Park and dispenses her own brand of justice. Angelina, the little heroine, experiences fear, indignation, helplessness, and a desire to inflict injury in order to halt a tribal assault on her person, but she has already developed a "larger sense of humanity" and cannot carry through on her threat. What she can, and does, do, is determine how to reward good behavior, because she knows, precociously, that a kiss freely given is a valued part of her self. In the child's world too, as Palacio Valdés observes, "all kinds of passions exist, from base envy to sublime heroism."

Noteworthy for compassion toward orphaned children and the bond established between an animal and a little person is "Polyphemus." Although this story borders on sentimentalism, it conveys the pain of abandonment and the scourge of abuse experienced by foundlings who are wards of the state and look for love and comfort in a sympathetic friend or an unquestioning animal. Andresito, an orphan who has been befriended by Muley (Polyphemus's dog) and who pays him back in his own coin, has been whipped by a cook at the asylum. He shows his canine friend his back and Palacio Valdés writes: "The dog, more compassionate than man, licked his livid flesh."

And it is a dog who gives rise to one of the most memorable stories written by Don Armando, as he was often called in his later years because of his benign and grandfatherly countenance. "A Witness for the Prosecution" is about a peculiar kind of abandonment, of a dog by a man, an abandonment so deeply felt by an animal that the human must question what his "humanity" stands for. After extending a hand of hope, the man fears inconvenience and becoming the butt of ridicule, which prompts him to opt for an ignoble way out: he hops on a passing streetcar. His cruelty causes him so much guilt that he fully expects to be held accountable on Judgment Day.

Most of the well-delineated, and credible, characters in Palacio Valdés's novels are women, from titular protagonists (Gloria, *Sister Saint Sulpice* and Marta, *Marta and María*) to principal figures (Clementina, *Foam* and Cecilia, *The Fourth Estate*). They are the personages who infuse the works with life, and with naturalness and spontaneity. Palacio Valdés also peoples his short stories with women who create unforgettable scenes: the coquettish young wife in "Seduction" flirting with the author; María, the adulteress of "Drama in the Flies" displaying more backbone than her pusillanimous lover; Clotilde holding her head high after being cruelly jilted in "Clotilde's Romance"; the abused wife Pepita listening to her husband recount his nefarious crime in "Bubbles"; and the smiling French girl in "Merci, Monsieur," lifting a man's spirit with a simple word of thanks. Moments—scenes of very human exchanges brought to life by very female characters.

Well might we ask what Armando Palacio Valdés, a nineteenth-century Spanish writer not in vogue, can offer to today's reader in English translation. And we might respond that he has the courage to take an optimistic view of life and make of it something other than a jeremiad. He understands that man is imperfect, flawed; he understands that life can be sorrow, suffering; but he also understands that we can wallow in misery or we can attempt to overcome it. In "The Bird in the Snow" Juan *wants* to triumph over adversity and it is not his blindness that defeats him, it is his fellow man's insensitivity, society's neglect. Much of the nature of literature is in the eye of the beholder, and if Palacio Valdés's roseate view makes his writings facile and superficial for some, for others this very sanguinity makes them uplifting and entertaining. The positive looms as large in life as the negative.

For this translation I have cross-checked two editions of Palacio Valdés's stories—the *Complete Works* in thirty-one volumes of the "edición definitivia" published by Fax (Madrid) in the late 1940s, and the seventh edition of the Works published by Aguilar (Madrid) in 1959.

I am deeply indebted to Millán Arroyo Simón, SJ, my friend and right hand in Madrid, for tracking down the heirs of Don Armando Palacio Valdés and securing authorization for me to publish in English translation the short stories that make up this book. And lastly, my thanks to Don Antonio Masip Hidalgo, former mayor of "the very noble and heroic city of Oviedo" ("Polyphemus"), whose generous gift of a detailed map of Asturias not only taught me some geography, but also kept me from making at least one egregious error.

*   *   *

Words and passages marked with an asterisk (*) in the text are explained in the Notes at the back of the book.

Armando Palacio Valdés

From left to right: José María de Pereda, Benito Pérez Galdós, Armando Palacio Valdés, Marcelino Menéndez Pelayo. Photo by Michael A. Micinilio.

Plaque on the front of Calle de Maldonado, 25, Madrid, where Armando Palacio Valdés lived the last twenty years of his life. Photo by Robert M. Fedorchek.

The Curate's Colt

Like me, many people have probably met the curate of Arbín*
and have had the opportunity to admire his kindly and highly
noble character, the simplicity of his habits, and a certain innocence of spirit that God grants only to those whom he has chosen. For these qualities he was esteemed and loved by all. He
lived in his rectory, which was at twice a stone's throw from the
town, attended by one elderly female servant and one male servant no less aged than she. He also had a mastiff, whom nobody
remembered as a pup, and a horse that had come into his hands
more than twenty years ago, and who was, according to the ex-
perts, over the hill. Since Don Pedro, the curate's name, was well
past seventy, it could rightly be said that his house was an an-
tique museum. We're going to tell the horse's story, leaving for
another occasion that of the mastiff, which is less interesting.

Nobody in the town knew him by any other name except "the
curate's colt." But, as the reader will understand, this was nothing more than a sobriquet that had been given to him to make
people laugh. The originator of such ridicule had to have been
Xuan de Manolín, who at the time was the most humorous, carefree spirit in the parish. The horse's real name was Pichón. This
was what his owner as well as the servants called him. In his
younger days he was dapple-gray, but when I first saw him he
had lost all the black streaks or they had turned white. He was
not bad looking and was gentle in nature, but his gait was only
moderately bouncy or swift. For years, therefore, the curate had
not dared to run him at a trot and preferred to leave a half hour
early on his outings to neighboring parishes. Patient, noble, reli-
able, and familiar with those roads like no one else, Pichón combined enough talents to be held in very high regard by his master.
The outstanding trait of this animal was, nevertheless, his frugal-
ity. Since the little grass that grew in the pasture land was all
eaten by a milk cow that the curate had, the unfortunate Pichón
was obliged for nine months of the year to wander along narrow

paths and alleyways watching for grass to grow in order to eat it much before it reached full height. No hack, young or old, ever looked out for himself with such a happy outcome because his hind quarters were always plump and shiny as if he were housed in the stable of some marquis. So much so that on more than one occasion the curate was asked if he fed him straw and barley. Barley for Pichón! The horse had heard some mention of it once, but see it—never.

As if these desirable traits were not sufficient, Pichón possessed another that was greatly prized: a prodigious memory. As soon as the curate of Arbín stopped once at any house in the surrounding area, the next time around Pichón would come to a clear halt in front of it as if inviting his master to dismount. Naturally if the house in question was that of the priest's sister, who lived in Felechosa, or that of the curate of El Pino, with whom Don Pedro had for many years been carrying on a permanent game of bezique, the horse not only stopped, he then went straight to the stable as well.

But Pichón had, without any reasonable motive, many enemies in the town, some of them overt, some of them covert. The latter, unable to find a way to take him on in an open fight, opposed him in a veiled, insidious crusade: they attacked him for his old age. As if all of us were not to reach it as a matter of course, the quadruped very rightly thought! They began by giving him that ludicrous nickname "colt." Pichón knew very well that he was not a colt, nor did he dream of acting like one. When had he ever been seen acting like a "dirty-minded old horse" or becoming prim and gay at the sight of a mare, for as featherbrained as she might be? Live honorably, never act hastily, eat what there was, not become involved in politics. These were the fundamental axioms that he had gleaned from his long experience.

Not satisfied with nicknaming him, his antagonists spread malicious lies about him. They said that once, going from Lena to Cabañaquinta, he had fallen asleep on the road while Don Pedro was riding him, and that it was necessary for a muleteer to thrash him to awaken him. Pure slander. What had happened was that at the house of the curate of Llanolatabla, where his master had spent nearly seven hours, they had not given him a single blade of grass, and, naturally, weakness caused him to fall. Likewise, witty neighbors, and many who were not so witty, indulged themselves in jokes on him that were in bad taste, and they never stopped teasing the priest about him. All of which caused Don Pedro, in spite of his well-known patience, to become extremely irritable at times. "Confound it!" he would grumble. "What can the poor animal have done to these blockheads for them to treat him so badly?"

The most relentless was Xuan de Manolín. The curate never rode by his tavern without seeing him come to the door to make one of his usual quips; if he didn't take Pichón by the bridle and act very polite at first, he would pull down his lip and ask with seeming innocence:

"Is he over the hill, Father?"

The customers, who also came to the door, rolled over in laughter on hearing this and similar gibes, and a miffed Don Pedro left fit to be tied.

Finally, he found himself so harassed by the continual raillery of his parishioners, in which his fellow parish priests from adjacent towns also took part when he met them at social affairs, that he determined to get rid of the horse, even though it might cause him considerable grief. Nevertheless, with the approach of the Feast of the Ascension fair, where he intended to sell him, he lost heart and came very close to changing his mind. But he had already stated his intentions in front of several of the townspeople. The whole parish knew of his decision and approved of it. What would they say if in the end he elected to keep Pichón?

One morning the curate, melancholy and distressed, mounted up and gradually made his way to Oviedo. As he approached the city, remorse gnawed at him more and more. For as much as he kept going over the idea, and even if numerous examples of this sort were cited, the truth is that it was singularly ungrateful to sell the beleaguered Pichón after twenty years of faithful service. Who knew what his fate would be! Perhaps pulling a diligence; perhaps dying iniquitously in a bullring. In any event, martyrdom. The innocence with which the animal walked, without fear or suspicion, produced a feeling of shame which his master was unable to repress.

Livestock was bringing in very little money at the fair and Pichón was so old that nobody wanted him. Only one horse-dealer offered fifteen *duros*. The curate finally let him go at this price fearful of the townspeople's ridicule if he showed up again with him in Arbín. After he had lost sight of Pichón, the curate calmed down because the presence of the quadruped made him suffer a great deal. He took the train home, and when he arrived he had the unpleasant experience of receiving congratulations for what he secretly considered a reprehensible act. A few days later, however, he had completely forgotten the horse.

But Don Pedro undoubtedly needed another one. Although he was in good health and had, thank the Lord, strong legs, some parishes were very distant and he could not always ask to borrow Xuan de Manolín's mare or Cosme the miller's stallion. On the advice of these and other knowledgeable parishioners, he decided against waiting for the All Saints' Day fair in Oviedo, preferring instead to look for a mount at the one held in San Pedro de Boñar, where almost all the horses in the province of León showed up.

Said and done. When the fair began, the curate availed himself of the mule of a muleteer friend of his who was going to León with his drove, and took the road to the village of Boñar by way of the San Isidro pass. There he encountered the opposite of what had been the case in Oviedo. The animals were expensive. For less than forty *duros* it was impossible to buy a horse worthy of the name. For forty-three and the customary gratuity that sealed a bargain, our curate became the owner of a sorrel not very lively in disposition, but so dependable and sure-footed that there was not another like him all along the banks of the Esla river, nor even those of the Orbigo, according to the dealers who sold him the animal. And that must have been the case, because Don Pedro remembered the Castilian saying: "The sorrel will sooner expire than tire."

Riding his new horse, the curate once again headed for home, passing through Lillo and Isoba and crossing the steep, narrow defiles of San Isidro. He rode along happy and satisfied with his purchase because the animal held up well on the rough hillside and, above all, did not become skittish, which was what the priest feared the most. But on arriving at Felechosa something happened that astonished him completely. And it was that while attempting to dismount for a moment at his sister's home, the horse went, on his own, straight to the stable.

"What a nose this animal has!" the curate exclaimed, entering the house.

And he was bubbling over with joy.

He stayed there too long and, considering how far he had to go, realized that it was impossible to stop at El Pino to play bezique with his priest friend. But on arriving there he experienced another and greater surprise. The horse, in spite of tugs on the noseband of the bridle and lashes from the switch, refused to follow the main road and, veering off it slightly, turned toward the priest's house and entered the stable.

"Incredible, by Jove, incredible!" muttered the curate, opening his eyes wide.

And because of that admirable instinct he lashed him no more and got down to say hello to his friend.

When he arrived at the town, it was late at night, for which reason the valuable and intelligent animal could not be seen and admired by the townspeople. But the following morning some of them appeared at the stable, and after seeing him they pronounced him a good horse and congratulated his master warmly for the purchase.

"The nag is *wunnerful*, Father! Now you have something to ride until the end of your days."

"It was about time you got rid of that old good-for-nothing, because when you come right down to it one of these days he would have left you on foot on the very road."

The curate was pleased to receive the congratulations, but the reminder of Pichón still made a painful impression on him.

After five or six days had gone by without Don Pedro having any need to ride his new horse, he instructed his male servant to groom and harness him because he intended to go to Mieres. The domestic came to him shortly afterwards and said:

"Do you know, Father, that León (which was the nag's name) has some white spots that won't go away?"

"Rub hard, numbskull, rub hard. He's probably grazed against a wall."

For as much as he tried, the servant could not get them to disappear. Angered, the curate then said to him:

"Face up to it, Manuel. You don't have the strength any more. Now you'll see them vanish in short order."

And, removing his cassock and rolling up his shirt sleeves, he himself took the brush and the scraper and began to rub León. But his efforts were for naught. The spots not only did not go away, but they were getting larger and larger.

"Let's see what this is. Bring some hot water and soap," he said finally, sweaty and irritated.

What a sight! The water was immediately dyed red, and the horse's white spots spread out to such an extent that they almost covered him. In a word, they scrubbed the animal so much that a half hour later the sorrel had disappeared and in his place was a white horse.

Manuel took a few steps backwards and, with consternation written all over his face, exclaimed:

"May God strike me dead if it isn't Pichón!"

The curate stopped in his tracks.

Sure enough, underneath the coat of red ochre or some other disgusting mixture with which they had disguised him, there was the old, patient, frugal, slandered Pichón.

The news spread through the town like wildfire. A short time later a number of people crowded together in front of the rectory studying, amid guffaws and jocular remarks, "the curate's colt," which the servant had brought out of the stable. At the height of their amusement, Don Pedro appeared on the porch with a stern, angry expression on his face and said:

"It serves me right, confound it, for having paid attention to some blockheads like you! I'll break the bones of whomever says another word to me about him. Confound it and confound it!"

Understanding that the curate had more than enough reason to be upset, there wasn't a peep from the onlookers, and they set off slowly toward the town.

Polyphemus*

Colonel Toledano, nicknamed *Polyphemus*, was a fierce, imposing man of gigantic stature who wore a long frock coat, checked
trousers, and a high hat with a very wide, turned-up brim; he
also had a stiff gait, enormous white moustache, thunderous
voice, and a heart of stone. But even more than this, the stern,
bloodthirsty look of his only eye inspired dread and horror. In
the war in Africa the one-eyed colonel had killed a great number
of Moors and had taken pleasure in pulling out their still pulsat-
ing entrails. At least this was what we kids blindly believed,
those of us who after school went to play at San Francisco Park
in the very noble and heroic city of Oviedo.

On clear days between twelve and two in the afternoon the
implacable warrior would also go there to take a walk. From a
great distance we caught a glimpse through the trees of his arro-
gant figure, which instilled terror in childish hearts, and when
we didn't make him out we heard his mighty voice resounding
through the foliage like a torrent rushing headlong.

The colonel was deaf too, and could only talk by shouting.

"I'm going to tell you a secret," he would say to whomever
accompanied him on his walk. "My niece Jacinta doesn't want
to marry Navarrete's boy."

And everybody within a quarter-mile radius learned about the
secret.

Generally he took his walk alone, but when some friend joined
him he considered it propitious. Perhaps he accepted the company willingly to have an opportunity to boom forth in his powerful voice. What's certain is that when he had an audience, San
Francisco Park shook. It was no longer a public walk; it formed
part of the colonel's exclusive dominions. The warbling of the
birds, the whispering of the wind, the sweet murmuring of the
fountain—everything fell silent. Only the imperious, authorita-
tive, stern shouting of the warrior of Africa was heard. To such
a degree that the cleric who accompanied him (at that time not

many clerics were accustomed to walking through the park) seemed to be there solely to open—first one, then another—all the registers that the colonel's voice possessed. How many times, hearing those terrible, thunderous shouts, seeing his angry manner and his fiery eye, did we think that he was going to pounce upon the miserable priest who had been improvident enough to join him!

This frightful man had a nephew who was about eight or ten, like us. Poor thing! We never saw him at the walk without feeling infinitely sorry for him. In the course of time I saw a tamer of wild beasts put a lamb in a lion's cage. It made the same impression on me as Gasparito Toledano walking with his uncle. We didn't understand how the miserable creature could retain his appetite and regularly perform his vital functions, how he didn't develop heart trouble or die, wasted by a slow fever. If a few days went by without his showing up at the park, the same doubt filled us with foreboding. "Can he have gobbled him up for a snack?" And when after all we found him safe and sound someplace, we experienced surprise and relief at the same time. But we were certain that sooner or later he'd end up being the victim of some bloodthirsty whim on the part of *Polyphemus*.

The strange thing about the situation was that Gasparito's lively face did not show the signs of terror and dejection that should have been the only ones stamped on it. On the contrary, there constantly shone in his eyes a hearty joy that amazed us. When he was with his uncle he walked with complete freedom of movement, smiling, happy, sometimes jumping up and down, other times walking decorously, his audacity or his ingenuousness going so far as to make faces at us behind his uncle's back. This produced the same painful effect on us as if we saw him dancing on the arrow atop the spire of the cathedral. "Gaspaar!" The air vibrated and transmitted that roar from one end of the walk to the other. There wasn't one of us there who didn't turn pale. Only Gasparito heeded the call as if he were being summoned by a siren. "What do you want, Uncle?" and he would approach him executing some complicated dance step.

Besides this nephew, the monster was owner of a dog that should have lived in the same misery, although it didn't seem to either. This dog was a big, beautiful, strong, swift great Dane with a blueish coat that answered to the name of *Muley*, doubtless in memory of some wretched Moor sacrificed by his master. *Muley*, like Gasparito, lived in *Polyphemus's* power the same as in an odalisque's lap. Funny, playful, friendly, incapable of duplicity—he was, without offending anybody, the least shy and the most approachable of all the dogs I've known in my life.

Whenever it was possible to do so, there being no danger that the colonel would notice, we used to fight for the honor of feeding him bread, biscuits, cheese, and other treats that our mothers gave us for a snack. *Muley* accepted it all with undisguised pleasure, and showed us unmistakable signs of affection and gratitude. But in order for the reader to see just how worthy and disinterested the feelings of this memorable canine were, and for him to serve as a lasting example to dog and man, I'll say that he didn't lavish the most affection on the one who treated him the most. A poor little orphan named Andrés usually played with us (in the provinces and at that time social classes didn't exist among children) and he couldn't give him anything because he didn't have anything. It didn't matter: *Muley* accorded him preferential treatment. The most insistent wags of his tail, the most pronounced and impetuous caresses were reserved for Andrés, to the detriment of the others. What an example for any representative of the political majority!

Did *Muley* sense that that destitute little boy, always silent and sad, needed his love more than the rest of us? I don't know, but it seemed that way.

For his part, Andresito had come to conceive a real passion for this animal. Whenever we were playing games in the highest part of the park and *Muley* unexpectedly showed up, it was a foregone conclusion: the dog would draw Andresito aside and spend a good while with him as if he had to share some secret. *Polyphemus's* colossal silhouette could be glimpsed through the distant trees.

But these hasty, anxiety-ridden meetings brought the orphan little satisfaction. Like one truly in love, he longed to enjoy the presence of his idol for a long time and alone.

Therefore one afternoon, with incredible boldness and under our very noses, he took the dog with him to the Poor House, as the Orphan Asylum is called in Oviedo, and didn't return for a full hour. His face was beaming with happiness; *Muley* also seemed elated. Fortunately, the colonel hadn't left the walk yet nor had he noticed his dog's desertion.

These getaways were repeated one afternoon after another. Andresito and *Muley's* friendship was growing stronger. Andresito would not have hesitated to give his life for *Muley.* If the opportunity had presented itself, I'm sure the latter would have done no less.

But the orphan still wasn't satisfied. He dreamed up the idea of taking *Muley* off to the Orphan Asylum to sleep with him. Being the cook's assistant, he slept in one of the corridors next to his room, on a wretched mattress of corn husks. One afternoon he led the dog to the Poor House and didn't return. What a delightful night for the miserable creature! Andresito hadn't known any caresses in his life except those of *Muley.* First his teachers, and afterwards the cook, had always spoken to him with a whip in their hands. They slept in an embrace like two lovers. Around dawn the little boy felt the smartness of a welt raised on his back by the cook's stick the previous afternoon. He took off his shirt.

"Look, *Muley,*" he said in a low voice, showing him the mark.

The dog, more compassionate than man, licked his livid flesh.

As soon as the doors were opened, Andresito let him out. *Muley* ran to his master's house, but in the afternoon he was back at the park, ready to follow the orphan. They slept together again that night, and the following one, and the next one too. But happiness in this world is short-lived, and Andresito was happy on the brink of disaster.

One afternoon, as we were all huddled together playing a game, we heard behind us two formidable reports.

"Stop, stop!"

Every head snapped around as if released by a spring. In front of us rose the Cyclopean figure of Colonel Toledano.

"Which one of you is the rapscallion who's abducting my dog every night? Out with it!"

A deathly silence greeted his question. We were transfixed with terror, rigid, as if made of stone.

Again the trumpet of the Last Judgment sounded.

"Who's the abductor? Who's the rascal? Who's the no-good . . .?"

Polyphemus's fiery eye devoured us one after another. *Muley,*

who accompanied him, was also looking at us, loyally, inno-
cently, and wagging his tail dizzily as a sign of uneasiness.

Then, Andresito, sallower than wax, advanced a step and said:

"Don't blame anyone, sir. It was me."

"How's that?"

"It was me," the boy repeated in a louder voice.

"So! It was you!" said the colonel, smiling fiercely. "And don't
you know to whom that dog belongs?"

Andresito remained silent.

"Don't you know whose it is?" he asked again at the top of his
voice.

"Yes, sir."

"How's that? Speak louder."

And he cupped his hand over his ear to form a trumpet.

"Yes, sir."

"Whose is it? Tell me."

"He's Mr. *Polyphemus's*."

I shut my eyes. I believe that my companions must have done
the same. When I opened them I expected that Andresillo would
already be erased from the book of the living. That wasn't the
case, fortunately. The colonel was staring at him, more curiously
than angrily.

"And why do you take him with you?"

"Because he's my friend and he loves me," the orphan said in
a firm voice.

The colonel stared at him again.

"All right," he said at last. "Well, see to it that you don't take
him anymore! If you do, be assured that I'll tear your ears off."

And he wheeled majestically on his heels. But before taking a
step he raised his hand to his vest, took out a half *duro*, and said,
turning back to Andresito:

"Here, buy yourself some candy. But see to it that you don't
make off with my dog again! I'm warning you!"

And off he went. Four or five paces away he happened to turn
around. Andresito had dropped the coin to the ground and was
sobbing, covering his face with his hands. The colonel came back
on the double.

"You're crying? Why? Don't cry, my boy."

"Because I love him a lot . . . , because he's the only one in the
world who loves me," Andrés whimpered.

"Well whose son are you?" asked the colonel, surprised.

"I'm from the Orphan Asylum."

"How's that?" *Polyphemus* shouted.

"I'm an orphan."

Then we saw the colonel change color. He rushed over to Andrés, separated his hands from his face, dried his tears with a handkerchief, and embraced him, and kissed him, saying emotionally:

"Forgive me, my boy, forgive me! Don't pay any attention to what I just said to you . . . Take the dog whenever you wish . . . Keep him with you as long as you want, do you understand? As long as you want . . ."

After he had calmed Andrés with these and other assurances, uttered in a tone of voice that took us by surprise, he headed again towards the walk, turning around repeatedly to shout to him:

"You can take the dog whenever you want, do you understand, my boy? Whenever you want . . ."

May God forgive me, but I'd swear that I saw a tear in *Polyphemus's* bloodshot eye.

Andresillo ran off, followed by his friend, who was barking with joy.

The Bird in the Snow

Juan was blind from birth and had been taught the only thing that blind people generally learn, music, a field in which he excelled. His mother died not many years after giving birth to him, and it had been just a year since the death of his father, a regimental bandmaster. His brother, who lived in South America, never wrote but word had reached Juan that he was married, had two lovely children, and held a good job. Indignant at this son's ingratitude, the father, while he lived, didn't want to hear his name, but the blind boy still regarded him very fondly. He couldn't help remembering that his brother, older than he, had been his haven in childhood, the defender of his weakness in the face of attacks by other children, and that this same brother always spoke to him affectionately. Santiago, on entering his room in the morning, would say, "Hello, Juanito! On your feet, man, don't sleep so much," and his voice sounded more pleasing and harmonious to the blind boy's ears than the keys of a piano and the strings of a violin. How had such a good person been transformed into a bad one? Juan refused to believe it and did everything in his power to excuse him. Sometimes he blamed the mail, other times he imagined that his brother didn't want to write until he could send a lot of money, and on occasion he thought that Santiago was going to surprise them some fine day, showing up with millions at the modest entresol where they lived, but he didn't dare mention these fanciful occurrences to his father. Only when the latter, exasperated, bitterly rebuked his absent son did Juan dare say to him: "Don't despair, Father. Santiago is a good person. I have a feeling that he's going to write one of these days."

The father, without seeing a letter from his older son, died while a priest exhorted him on one side and the poor blind boy convulsively squeezed his hand on the other, as if it were a question of retaining him in this world by force. When they attempted to remove the body from the house, Juan engaged in

31

a frightful, frantic struggle with the funeral home employees. Finally, he ended up alone, but what aloneness his was! No father, no mother, no relatives, no friends; he didn't even have the sun, the friend of all of God's creatures. He spent two days shut up in his room, pacing it from one end to the other like a caged wolf, refusing to eat. At long last the maid, helped by a compassionate neighbor woman, managed to prevent his suicide. He began to eat again and from that point on spent the rest of his life praying and playing the piano.

Some time before his death, the father had succeeded in securing Juan an appointment as organist in one of Madrid's churches, a position that paid three *pesetas* a day. It wasn't enough, understandably, to maintain a home, as modest as it might be, so after a fortnight Juan sold the humble belongings of his dwelling for a small amount, a meager amount actually, discharged the maid and went off to a rooming house as a boarder for two *pesetas* a day. The remaining *peseta* sufficed to meet his other needs. For several months Juan lived without setting foot in the street except to go play the organ: he went from the house to the church and from the church to the house. Sorrow engulfed and disheartened him to such an extent that he scarcely uttered a word. He spent his time composing a special requiem Mass that he counted on having played in memory of his deceased father through the intercession of the parish priest. And since it couldn't be said that he brought all five senses to bear on his opus, because he was missing one, we can and will say that he devoted himself to it heart and soul.

The change of government surprised him before he had completed it. I don't know if the radicals, the conservatives or the constitutionalists took over, but a new group did take over. Juan didn't find out until it was late and to his detriment. After a few days the new cabinet determined that he was an organist who represented a danger to public order, and that from the height of. the choir he engaged in a truly scandalous opposition to it by booming and buzzing on every one of the organ's stops at vespers and high Masses. Since the incoming government refused, as it had stated in Congress through one of its most prominent members, "to tolerate any outside interference," it proceeded immediately and with salutary energy to dismiss Juan, looking for a substitute who exhibited more reliability in his musical operations and showed more loyalty to the establishment. On being notified of his dismissal, the blind boy experienced nothing except surprise; deep down he was almost glad because they were allowing him more free time to complete his Mass. He only grasped his situation clearly when at the end of the month the landlady appeared in his room to ask him for money. Juan didn't have it because he no longer earned wages at the church; he needed to pawn his father's watch to pay the rent. Afterwards he was as calm as before and continued composing without worrying about the future. But again the landlady asked him for money, and again Juan was obliged to pawn an article—a diamond ring—from the very scant paternal inheritance; finally, he had nothing left to pawn. Then, out of consideration for his disability, they accommodated him a few more days—very few—as a courtesy, and afterwards closed their doors to him, priding themselves greatly on letting him keep his trunk and clothing, since with the latter they could have recovered the little bit that he owed them.

Juan found another house but couldn't rent a piano, which saddened him deeply; he could no longer finish his Mass. He still went for some time to the home of a friend who owned a warehouse and played the piano once in a while. He soon realized, however, that he was less and less welcome, and stopped going there.

Not long afterwards he was thrown out of the new house, but this time his trunk was kept as security. There then began such a miserable and agonizing period for the blind boy that few will fully comprehend the suffering, better yet, the torment meted out by fate. Bereft of friends, clothing, and money, there is no doubt that one has a very difficult time of it in the world, but if added to this is not seeing sunlight, and being absolutely helpless as a result, we'll scarcely manage to perceive the extent of his grief and misery. Going from inn to inn only to be thrown out of all of them shortly after having entered; getting in bed so that the only shirt he owned could be washed; wearing torn shoes and trousers frayed at the bottom; in need of a haircut and shave, nobody knows how long Juan wandered around Madrid. He sought, through one of the boarders who showed more compassion than the others, the position of pianist at a café. It was finally given to him only to be taken away a few days later. Juan's music didn't find favor with the customers of the Cebada Café. He didn't play *jotas, polos, sevillanas** or flamenco rhythms, not even polkas; he would spend the evenings performing sonatas by Beethoven and concertos by Chopin. The people present would despair at not being able to beat time with their teaspoons.

Again the wretched youth wandered through the most squalid areas of the capital. Some charitable souls, who learned of his sorry state by chance, would aid him indirectly, because Juan shuddered at the idea of begging. At a tavern in the slums he ate the bare minimum to keep from starving to death, and for fifteen centimes spent nights amidst beggars and malefactors in an attic rented solely for sleeping. On one occasion he was robbed of his trousers while asleep, and others of mended drill were left for him. It was the month of November.

Poor Juan had always fantasized that his brother would return, and overcome now by adversity, he began to nourish the dream eagerly. He had somebody write to him in Havana, although without putting the address on the letter because he didn't know it; he tried to learn if anyone had seen him, but to no avail; and every day he spent a few hours on his knees asking God to bring him to his aid. The unfortunate creature's only happy moments were the ones that he spent in prayer in the corner of some solitary church. Concealed behind a pillar, breathing the pungent odors of wax and dampness, listening to the sputtering of candles and the faint murmur of the prayers of the few worshippers scattered throughout the nave and aisles of the temple, his innocent soul would leave this world, which treated him so cruelly, and rise to commune with God and His Most Holy Mother. Since childhood Juan had professed a deeply-rooted, heartfelt devotion to the Virgin. Because he had barely known his own mother, he instinctively sought in God's the tender, loving protection that only a woman can give to a child; in her honor he had composed some hymns and prayers, and never went to sleep without kissing devoutly the scapulary of Our Lady of Mt. Carmel* that he wore around his neck.

There came a day, nevertheless, when heaven and earth deserted him. Refused admittance everywhere, without a single piece of bread to eat and without clothing to ward off the cold, the destitute musician realized with terror that the moment of begging was at hand. A desperate struggle took place in the depths of his spirit. Misery and shame contested the terrain inch by inch with necessity; the darkness that enveloped him made the fight even more agonizing. In the end, as was to be expected, hunger triumphed. After spending many hours sobbing and asking God for the strength to bear his misfortune, Juan resolved to appeal to charity, but he still tried to mask his humiliation, and decided to sing in the streets only at night. He possessed a fairly good voice and knew the art of singing to perfection, but he ran into the problem of not having a way to accompany himself. Finally, another poor devil, not as down-and-out as he, provided him with an old, broken guitar, and after fixing it as best he could, and after shedding copious tears, he went out into the street one December night. His heart was pounding and his legs were trembling. When he attempted to sing in one of the more central streets he couldn't: misery and shame had produced a lump in his throat. Juan leaned against the wall of a house, rested a few moments and, somewhat recovered, began to sing the tenor's *romanza* from the first act of "La Favorita."* A blind boy who wasn't singing *peteneras* and *malagueñas** caught the attention, naturally, of passersby, and many of them formed a circle around him; several, on noting the skill with which he overcame the difficulties of the piece, quietly communicated to each other their surprise and left a little money in the hat that he had hung on his arm. At the conclusion of the *romanza*, Juan began the aria from the fourth act of "L'Africaine."* But too many people had gathered around him, and the authorities feared that this might be the cause of some disorder, because for policemen it's axiomatic that people who gather together in the street to listen to a blind boy demonstrate by this act dangerous instincts of rebellion and hostility towards institutions, an attitude, in short, incompatible with social order and the safety of the State. For which reason a policeman took Juan firmly by the arm and said to him:

"All right go on back to your home right now and don't stop in any other street."

"But I'm not harming anybody."

"You're blocking traffic. Move on, move on, if you don't want to go to the police station."

It's really comforting to see the great care exercised by government authorities to ensure that public thoroughfares always be free of blind beggars who sing. And I believe, though there may be some who maintain the contrary, that if they could keep them equally free of thieves and murderers, they would do so gladly.

Poor Juan returned to his filthy lodgings distressed, because he was good-hearted, at having momentarily endangered internal peace and given the state cause to intervene. He had earned sufficient money to eat the next day and pay for use of the miserable straw mattress on which he slept. At night he went out again to sing opera selections and sundry songs. Once more people gathered around him and once more the police intervened, shouting at him forcefully:

"Move on, move on."

But if he moved on, he wouldn't earn a penny because the passersby wouldn't hear him! Nevertheless, Juan always kept walking, for what made him shudder, more than the thought of death, was the idea of disregarding the injunctions of authorities and disturbing, albeit briefly, public order.

Each night his earnings dwindled. On the one hand, it was the necessity of always staying on the move, and on the other, it was the lack of novelty, which always costs one very dear in Spain, and this deprived him of a few centimes every day. With the ones that he did bring home he had barely enough to buy himself something to keep from starving to death. His situation was now desperate. The poor devil continued to cling tenaciously to the only bright spot in the darkness of his distress. This bright spot was the arrival of his brother Santiago. Every night, on going out with his guitar around his neck, the same thought occurred to him: If Santiago were in Madrid and heard me sing he'd recognize me by my voice. And this hope or, rather, pipe dream, was the only thing that gave him the strength to endure life.

There came another day, nevertheless, when anguish and pain knew no limits. The previous night he had earned only twenty centimes. It had been so cold! Understandably, for Madrid awoke wrapped in a blanket of snow about four inches deep. And it kept on snowing all day long without stopping for an instant, which didn't worry most people, and was cause for joy among many devotees of esthetics. Poets who enjoyed a comfortable position spent, more than most, the greater part of the day watching the falling snowflakes through the windows of their studies and pondering elegant, ingenious similes of the kind that makes the-

ater audiences shout "Bravo, bravo!" or obliges one to exclaim
when reading them in a volume of verse, "What talent this young
man has!"

The only nourishment that Juan had had was a cup of vile
coffee and a roll. He couldn't stave off hunger by contemplating
the beauty of the snow—in the first place because he was sight-
less, and in the second, because even if he weren't, it was unlikely
that he could see through the dirty, foggy barred window of his
attic. He spent the day huddled up on his mattress, remembering
the days of his childhood and clinging to the sweet mania of his
brother's return. As night fell, Juan felt faint and, pressed by
necessity, went down to the street to ask for alms. He no longer
had a guitar; he had sold it for three *pesetas* in a similar moment
of want.

The snow was falling with the same steadiness—with the same
vengeance, one could say. The pitiful musician's legs were
trembling just like the first day that he went out to sing, but this
time it was from hunger rather than shame. He trudged as best
he could through the streets, sinking in slush above his ankles.
His ear told him that hardly any pedestrians were passing by, and
since the carriages weren't making any noise he was in danger of
being run over by one. In a central street he finally began to sing
the first opera selection that came to his mind. His voice sounded
hoarse and weak; nobody approached him, not even out of curiosity. "Let's go somewhere else," Juan said to himself, and headed
down San Jerónimo Avenue, walking slowly through the snow,
his body cloaked in a mantle of white and his feet splashing
slush. The chill was penetrating his bones, and hunger was giving him a bad stomachache. There came a moment in which the
cold and pain got so severe that he almost fell unconscious; he
thought he was dying, and raising his spirit to Our Lady of Mt.
Carmel, his protectress, Juan exclaimed in an anguished voice:
"Help me, my mother!" And after pronouncing these words, he
felt a little better and walked, or more accurately, dragged himself
to Cortes Square. There he leaned against the post of a street
lamp, and, still under the influence of Our Lady's intercession,
began to sing Gounod's *Ave Maria*, a melody for which he had
always had a predilection. But nobody approached him there
either. All of the city's inhabitants were gathered together in cafés
and theaters, or else in their homes bouncing their children on

their knees near the fire. The snow continued falling slowly and copiously, determined to afford all newspaper reporters the subject matter with which to create a dozen well-turned phrases and delight their devoted readers the following day. Pedestrians who happened to pass by did so hurriedly, wrapped up in their capes and shielding themselves with umbrellas. The street lamps had put on their white night caps and let a melancholy light trickle out. No noise at all was heard except the muted, distant sound of carriages and the incessant falling of snowflakes reminiscent of an extremely faint and prolonged rustling of silks. Only Juan's voice vibrated in the silence of the night, saluting the Mother of the Unprotected. And his singing, more than a hymn of salutation, sometimes seemed like a shout of anguish, while other times it resembled a sorrowful, resigned groan that froze the heart more than the coldness of the snow.

In vain did the blind boy clamor for a long time, beseeching heaven's help; in vain did he repeat endlessly the sweet name of Mary, adapting it to the different strains of the melody. Heaven and the Virgin were, apparently, far away, and did not hear him; the residents of the square were near by, but refused to hear him. Nobody came down to take him in and no balcony opened even to toss him a copper coin. Pedestrians, as if they were being pursued by pneumonia, didn't dare to stop.

Finally, Juan couldn't sing any longer; his voice was dying in his throat, his legs were buckling, and he was losing sensation in his hands. He took a few steps and sat on the sidewalk at the foot of the iron fence that surrounds the garden. With his elbows on his knees and his head between his hands, Juan thought vaguely that the last moments of his life had arrived and again he prayed fervently and implored divine mercy.

After a while he believed that he sensed a pedestrian stopping in front of him, and felt himself taken by the arm. He raised his head and, suspecting that it would be the usual thing, asked timidly:

"Are you a policeman?"

"I'm not a policeman," replied the pedestrian, "but get up."

"I can barely make it, sir."

"Are you very cold?"

"Yes, sir . . . and besides, I haven't eaten today."

"Then I'll help you. Come on . . . up!"

The gentleman took Juan by the arms and stood him up; he was strong.

"Now lean firmly on me and let's see if we find a carriage."

"But where are you taking me?"

"No place bad. Are you afraid?"

"Oh, no! Something tells me that you're a charitable person."

"Let's be on the move and see if we can get home quickly for you to dry off and eat something hot."

"God will repay your kindness, sir . . . and the Virgin too . . . I thought I was going to die there."

"Don't say anything about dying . . . Don't talk about that anymore. The important thing now is finding a carriage right away. Let's keep moving . . . What's this? You're stumbling?"

"Yes, sir. I believe I've bumped into the post of a street lamp . . . Because I am blind!"

"You're blind?" the stranger asked eagerly.

"Yes, sir."

"Since when?"

"Since birth."

Juan felt his protector's arm tremble, and they continued walking in silence. Finally, the stranger stopped a moment and asked him in an agitated voice:

"What's your name?"

"Juan."

"Juan what?"

"Juan Martínez."

"Your father was Manuel, right? Bandmaster of the third artillery regiment, correct?"

"Yes, sir."

At that very same moment the blind boy felt himself clutched tightly by strong arms that almost suffocated him and heard in his ear a shaky voice that exclaimed:

"My God, what horror and what happiness! I'm a criminal, I'm your brother Santiago."

And the two brothers stood embracing and sobbing for several minutes in the middle of the street. The snow was falling on them gently.

Santiago abruptly disengaged himself from his brother's arms and began to shout, interlarding his words with strong oaths:

"A carriage, a carriage! Aren't there any carriages around here?

Damn my luck! Come on, Juanillo, make an effort . . . we'll be home soon. But where have the carriages gone? Not a one is passing by . . . I see one over there . . . Thank God! What? The fool is going further away! Here's another . . . this one's mine. All right, driver; five *duros* if you take us on the double to the Castellana, number ten."

And taking his brother in his arms as if he were a child, Santiago set him inside the carriage and then climbed in behind. The driver urged the horse on and the vehicle glided swiftly and noiselessly over the snow. While they sped along, Santiago, always clasping his pitiful brother, told him quickly about his life. He hadn't been in Cuba, but Costa Rica, where he put together a respectable fortune; but he had spent many years out in the country, having hardly any communication with Europe. He had sent three or four letters by the boats that traded with England and never received a reply. And since he was always planning to return to Spain the next year, he stopped making inquiries with the intention of giving them a pleasant surprise. Afterwards he married, and this event delayed his return considerably. But he had been in Madrid for four months now and learned from the parish register that their father had died. People gave him vague and contradictory information concerning Juan: some told him that he had died too, while others said that, reduced to utter poverty, he had begun to sing and play the guitar in the streets. All the efforts that he made to ascertain his brother's whereabouts were futile. Fortunately, Providence took it upon itself to bring Juan into his arms. As he spoke Santiago sometimes laughed and sometimes cried, always displaying the open, generous, jovial disposition that he had had as a child.

The carriage finally stopped. A servant came to open the door and they whisked Juan to the house. Upon entering, he perceived a tepid temperature—the aroma of well-being that's spread by wealth—and his feet sunk in soft carpeting. On Santiago's order, two servants immediately stripped Juan of his drenched rags and put clean, warm clothing on him. He was then served, in the very sitting room where a delightful fire was blazing, a cup of soothing broth followed by some solid food, although with the proper caution due to the weak condition that his stomach must have been in. The most exquisite old wine, moreover, was brought up from the wine cellar. Santiago didn't stop moving about, issuing timely orders, constantly approaching his blind brother to ask him anxiously:

"How do you feel, Juan? Are you comfortable? Do you want another glass of wine? Are you warm enough?"

Once Juan had finished his light repast, both brothers remained beside the fireplace for a few moments. Santiago asked a servant if the lady of the house and the children were already in bed, and having been told that they were, he said to Juan, overflowing with joy:

"Don't you play the piano?"

"Yes."

"Well, let's give my wife and children a scare. Come into the parlor."

And he led Juan to the piano and sat him down. Then he raised the top so that the sound might be heard better, opened the doors carefully, and performed all the maneuvers conducive to producing a surprise in the house; but he did all of it with such great care—walking on tiptoe, speaking in falsetto, and making so many and such funny faces—that Juan, on sensing it, couldn't help laughing and exclaimed:

"You're always the same, Santiago!"

"Now play, Juanillo, play with all your strength."

The blind musician began to perform a military march. The quiet villa suddenly shook, like a music box when it's wound. The notes crowded one another as they flowed from the piano, but always with a martial rhythm. Now and then Santiago would exclaim:

"Louder, Juanillo, louder!"

And each time Juan pounded the keyboard with greater vigor.

"I see my wife now behind the curtains . . . Keep it up, Juanillo, keep it up . . . ! The poor thing's in her nightgown . . . ha . . . ha . . . I'm pretending that I don't see her . . . She's going to think that I'm mad . . . ha . . . ha! Keep it up, Juanillo, keep it up!" Juan obeyed his brother, although unwillingly now, because he wished to meet his sister-in-law and kiss his niece and nephew.

"Now I see my daughter Manolita, who's also dressed in a nightgown . . . Well, I'll be, Paquito has also awakened! Didn't I tell you that all of them were in for a good scare? But they're going to catch cold if they walk around like that much longer. Don't play any more, Juan, don't play any more."

The infernal din stopped.

"All right, Adela, Manolita, Paquito—put something on to keep warm and come and embrace my brother Juan, about whom I've spoken to you so much, whom I've just found in the street on the point of freezing to death in the snow . . . Come on, get dressed quickly."

Santiago's noble family came immediately to embrace the poor blind boy. His brother's wife's voice was sweet and gentle—Juan thought he was listening to the Virgin, and he heard her cry when her husband related how he had found him. And Adela even tried to add to the attention showered on him by Santiago: she ordered a footwarmer brought in, wrapped his legs in a blanket, and put a velvet cap on his head. The children hovered around the armchair, caressing their uncle and being caressed by him. They all listened in silence—and overcome with emotion—to the brief account that Juan gave them of his misfortune. Santiago was pounding his head; his wife was crying; and his children, astounded, said to Juan while grasping his hand:

"You won't be hungry again or go out into the street without an umbrella, will you, Uncle? I don't want you to: Manolita doesn't want you to either; nor Papa, nor Mama."

"I'll bet you won't let him have your bed, Paquito," said Santiago, instantly turning happy.

"He don't fit in it, Papa! In the other room there's a real, real, real big one . . ."

"I don't want a bed now," Juan interrupted. "I'm so comfortable here!"

"Does your stomach ache as it did before?" Manolita asked, embracing him and kissing him.

"No, my child, it doesn't. Bless you! It doesn't ache at all . . . I'm very happy. The only thing the matter with me is that I'm sleepy; my eyes are closing on me without my being able to prevent it."

"Well, don't keep from going to sleep on our account, Juan," said Santiago.

"Yes, Uncle, sleep, sleep," Manolita and Paquito said at the same time, throwing their arms around him and hugging him.

* * *

And, in fact, Juan did fall asleep. And he awoke in heaven.

At dawn the following day a police officer stumbled upon a corpse in the snow. The doctor in the emergency room certified that he had frozen to death.

"Look, Jiménez," one of the policemen who had brought Juan there said to his companion. "It looks like he's laughing!"

Drama in the Flies

I

According to all the backstage personnel, Antoñico was a live wire. Nobody had known a callboy like him in many a year. One needed to go back to the times of Máiquez and Rita Luna,* which was done with some frequency by a stout gentleman who went to the lounge every night to chat, to find a model of such intelligence and activity.

Only when he died were his services appreciated for what they were worth, because he wasn't the ordinary callboy who makes the rounds of actors' and actresses' dressing rooms five minutes beforehand shouting: "Don José, you're almost on" or "Miss Clotilde, whenever you're ready." Absolutely not. Antoñico had at his fingertips all the details indispensable to the smooth flow of the performance. He directed the stage machinery with admirable precision, gave timely advice to the propman, and had the curtain lowered without ever lagging behind or beginning prematurely. When there was a need to sound bells to imitate the noise of a carriage, he sounded them; if a whistle had to be blown, he blew it; and he even played a drumroll with amazing skill, deadening the sound to make the audience believe that the soldiers were withdrawing. In the plays in which the mob arrived in a rage at the doors of the palace and threatened to plunder it, he was unmatched in making a lot of noise with but a handful of people. He needed only a dozen extras to terrify the royal family: he would have one shout continuously, *Enough already!*; he would order a second to yell without stopping, *Death to the tyrants!*; a third, *Down with the chains!*; etc., etc., all in a perfectly executed crescendo that instilled terror not only in the hearts of the tyrants, but also in the hearts of all those who took an interest in their fate. Besides, he knew how to throw stones on to the stage so that they would make a lot of noise but not harm anyone. Sometimes he also projected his voice from the

44

wings or from below the stage in the capacity of a ghost. In short, more than a callboy, Antoñico ought to be considered an eminent, although invisible, actor.

In the theater he was almost a dictator. Actors and actresses flattered him because he could do them mischief with an intentional oversight; the management appeared to be content with him and the employees respected him and considered him their boss.

One had to see him with a reflector in his right hand, the playbook in his left, and a red Catalan cap on his head in the manner of a uniform, slipping swiftly through the wings, moving from one end of the theater to the other in a flash, hurrying the workmen, answering the thousand and one questions put to him, and dispatching orders in telegraphic style like a general in the roar of battle.

II

Notwithstanding the above, Antoñico had a serious shortcoming: an excessive attraction to women. Perhaps you'll say that this isn't a serious shortcoming. Were it any other man I would agree, but in Antoñico, a theater employee of such importance, it was a mortal sin. One has only to take into account that under his immediate purview were several supporting actresses, or rather, bit players, and that even lead actresses were obliged to be in constant contact with him. From which situation there frequently arose a number of vexations and excesses that would have been avoided if the callboy had a less inflammable disposition. For example: the theater would have avoided the departure of Narcisa, the young actress who played the role of working-class girls and who raised a ruckus, saying to whomever wanted to listen to her, that Antoñico pinched actresses' legs at propitious moments; it would have also avoided the charge made by the mother of Clotilde, the leading lady, who complained to the manager that Antoñico was too quick to lift up her daughter whenever the latter fainted at the end of an act. One has to agree that all this was unbecoming and harmed in no small measure the respectability of the callboy, who, I repeat, was beyond the shadow of a doubt the life and soul of the theater.

Such was the state of affairs when the chief stagehand married in the middle of the season. He was an ugly, taciturn, sullen man of about thirty with deep-set black eyes and a sparse, bristly beard; he was knowledgeable about everything and conscientious about his work. The woman that he chose for his wife had an upturned nose and was pretty, vivacious, high-spirited, lazy, as playful as a kitten, and very young, almost a child. She married the stagehand . . . I don't know why—maybe for his well-paying job (he earned six *pesetas* a day).

The uxorious husband brought her to the theater with him so as not to go without her company for a moment. In the brief periods that his responsibilities left him free, the poor devil enjoyed approaching his young wife and pinching her or giving her a furtive embrace. The girl, who until then hadn't set foot in the backstage world, was amazed and pleased to be in the midst of that bustle, and it soon became a necessity to spend three or four nights a week wandering through the wings and dressing rooms of the actresses, with whom she hit it off immediately.

Antoñico, on seeing her for the first time, licked his chops like the tiger that spies his prey. The red Catalan cap suffered a strong tremor and prepared to harbor a swarm of sinister, lecherous thoughts. But, like a cautious, experienced man, he guarded his ideas—at odds with family unity—under his Catalan cap and pretended not to notice the prey and let her calmly come and go whenever she wished.

Nevertheless, on running into her in corridors, he would occasionally direct magnetic glances at her, glances that fascinated her, and utter "Good evenings" fraught with ruinous intentions. Naturally, the stagehand's pretty wife did not fail to entertain suspicions about the nature of the thoughts that were hidden inside the Catalan cap, and accordingly she decided to blush all over whenever she came across the tiger-callboy. The latter proceeded with caution, step by step. No pinches, no stupid swearwords, no squeezes against the wings: a calm, gentle, almost melancholy attitude, calculated not to scare the game away; a few honeyed, furtive little words; several flattering little figures of speech couched in sighs; and when the groundwork was properly laid—Bang!—the quick move familiar to all. "María, I'm crazy about you. Forgive my boldness. I can't hold back any longer what I feel for you." Etc., etc.

The stagehand's vivacious wife fell, as was to be expected,

into the callboy's clutches. And there began for both a period of bittersweet pleasures, happiness along with trepidation. Pretending not to look at each other, they didn't take their eyes off each other; feigning that they barely knew each other, they were always together! And the husband was so sullen, so suspicious! They needed to implement marvels of strategy not to be found out. Sometimes four or five evenings would go by without their being able to exchange a single word. Racking his brain for ideas, Antoñico dreamed up the most stupendous and fantastic meetings—sometimes they were in the basement, other times in the dressing room of an actor who was on stage, but they were all brief and hectic because the stagehand, like a typical newly-wed husband, stayed close, and Antoñico only assumed his tigerish appearance with women.

One evening when the callboy, due to the unavoidable abstinence of many days, felt more in love than other times, he quickly whispered a few words in María's ear and disappeared among the wings. She followed him. They met in a dark corner near the front curtain, and the callboy, who knew every inch of those recesses, reached out to his paramour with one hand, separated a wing with the other, and the two of them slipped into a cramped little opening formed by curtains and wings. Antoñico drew towards himself the wing that he had separated and they ended up completely enclosed. The lovers were able to enjoy fleeting moments of safety which the callboy's experience and cleverness had sought. In that odd retreat nobody could find them. Nobody? Antoñico saw unexpectedly, at the height of their rapture, that an eye was observing them through a small hole opened in the curtain, and his tiger's heart began to throb violently. "María," he said in a shaky, imperceptible voice, "we're finished . . . , someone's watching us . . . Quiet! Will you go out first?" The stagehand's spirited wife abruptly pulled the wing aside and stepped forward. Nobody was there. Antoñico came out behind her, his face exhibiting an interesting pallor. Their first concern was looking everywhere for the stagehand. They found him extremely preoccupied, because the marble chimney slated to appear in the third act had been broken in transit; so absorbed was he that he took no heed of his wife when she approached him.

"Do you see," María said to Antoñico, "what a chicken you are? Fear is making you see things."

III

Quite a few days passed. The adulterous relations of our hero and heroine followed the same course, simultaneously sweet and stormy: fear, anxiety, worry, constant vacillation; presents, intense pleasures, and moments of happiness, in spite of everything. Such is the lot of illegitimate passion. María had completely forgotten the episode of the hole in the curtain; Antoñico still dreamed occasionally about that fantastic, scrutinizing eye, and would awake terrified. Little by little he became convinced that it had been an illusion brought on by fear, and fear made way for confidence.

One night the stagehand spoke to him as follows:

"Listen, Antoñico. Don't you think that the third curtain, the one with the columns, ought to be placed further back?"

"Why?"

"There's no perspective."

"Sure there is . . . , and besides, it would almost run into the lake."

"The lake can also be drawn back a little."

"There's no room."

"We still have about four and a half feet."

"How can we have that much? Have you measured it?"

"Yes, I've measured it. Do you have a ruler there? Then come take a look and see for yourself."

The stagehand started up and Antoñico followed him. They climbed the narrow, wobbly ladder that led to the flies. When he was halfway up, the stagehand turned around and his eyes met the callboy's. What was so remarkable about the former's gaze? Why did Antoñico's face turn pale? Why did his legs give way?

For a moment he hesitated whether to continue or turn back; the red Catalan cap stopped and flapped, prey to a fatal uncertainty. The stagehand exclaimed:

"Devil of a ladder! I climb it seventy times a day and I never get used to it. I'll die of a heart attack, Antoñico, I'll die of a heart attack."

The callboy regained his courage and continued to climb.

IV

That night they were performing a historical play set in the time of the Goths. The leading man was a very congenial youth, overflowing with enthusiasm and ten-line stanzas in the manner of Calderón.* The leading lady wore a very long tunic and would begin to cry from the very moment that the curtain was being raised. The actor who did old men's parts played the king and was supposed to die at the end of the third act, at the hands of the youth of the ten-line stanzas; he possessed a good voice, powerful and deep, as befitted a Visigothic king.

The audience impatiently awaited the catastrophe. When they felt like it, they yawned; when they thought it necessary, they produced newspapers and read them. There were many people who came to wish that the Visigothic king would soon keel over awash with blood in order for them to hurry home and get in bed.

In the second act there was a monologue of unwonted length recited by the king. The audience had already sat through seventy-five octosyllables of it and was getting ready to listen with resignation to another round equally as long, when all of a sudden . . .

"What's happened? What's going on? Why is the audience standing up? Why is the stage filling with people?"

A shape—a man—had just fallen from the flies onto the stage with a frightful crash. A group of people surrounded him immediately. The audience, terrified, got excited and made a racket; they wanted to know what had happened. At length an actor stepped away from the group and said in a loud voice ". . . that the callboy Antonio García, while walking along the gridiron, had had the misfortune to fall off."

"But is he dead? Is he dead?" several onlookers asked.

The actor signaled affirmatively with his head.

The Crime on Perseguida Street

"Yes, sir. You're looking at a murderer."

"What do you mean, Don Elías?" I asked, laughing as I filled his glass with beer.

Don Elías is the kindest, the most forbearing and the most disciplined individual in the Telegraph Corps, incapable of going out on strike even if the director ordered him to brush his trousers.

"Yes, sir . . . , there are circumstances in life . . . , there comes a moment when even the most peaceful of men . . ."

"Is that so? Tell me about it," I said, my curiosity aroused.

"It was in the summer of '78. Due to the reform I had ended up on leave, and I went to O . . . to stay with a married daughter who lives there. My life was too good: I ate, took walks, and slept. Occasionally I helped my son-in-law, who was employed in the town hall, to copy the secretary's minutes. We ate dinner without fail at eight o'clock. After putting my granddaughter to bed, who at the time was three years old and today is a lively young blond on the plump side, of the kind that appeals to you (modestly I lowered my eyes and took a drink of beer), I would go off to have my usual evening chat with Doña Nieves, a widow who lived alone on Perseguida Street and to whom my son-in-law owed his job. She lived in her own home, a big, old house with a dark exterior patio door and stone stairs. Don Gerardo Piquero, who had been Customs Collector in Puerto Rico and was retired, usually went there too. He died two years ago, the poor man. He got there at nine; I never arrived until after nine-thirty. On the other hand, at exactly ten-thirty he would leave, while I was accustomed to staying until eleven or a little later.

"One night I said good-bye, as usual, at about that time. Doña Nieves was very economical and lived like a poor person, even though she possessed enough property to indulge herself and live like a woman of means. She had no light whatsoever to illuminate the stairs and hallway. When Don Gerardo or I left, the maid would light our way from above with an oil lamp from the kitchen. As soon as we closed the hallway door, she closed the interior door and left us in almost total darkness, because very little light shone from the street.

"As I took my first step I felt what's commonly called a cuff; what I mean is that with a strong blow my top hat was knocked down to my nose. I was paralyzed by fear and fell against the wall. I thought I heard laughter, and somewhat recovered from my fright I pulled off my hat.

"'Who's there?' I said, making my voice sound formidable and threatening.

"Nobody responded. Several possibilities quickly passed through my mind. Would they try to rob me? Did some vagabonds want to amuse themselves at my expense? Was it possibly a friend playing a joke? I resolved to get out of there immediately because the doorway was clear. When I had gone halfway down the hall someone slapped me sharply on the buttocks with the palm of his hand, and at the same time a group of five or six men blocked the door. 'Help!' I shouted in a muffled voice, backing away again toward the wall. The men started to jump up and down in front of me making faces in a wild manner. My terror had reached its height.

"'Where are you going at this hour, you thief?' one of them said.

"'He's probably going to rob some dead man. He's the doctor,' another one said.

"Then the suspicion that they were drunk crossed my mind, and recovering, I exclaimed forcefully:

"'Out of my way, riffraff! Let me by or I'll kill somebody.'

"At the same time I brandished the iron cane that was given to me by a master arms maker and that I was accustomed to carrying at night.

"The men, without paying attention, continued dancing around in front of me and making the same crazy faces. I could see in the faint light that shone from the street that they kept putting in front one who seemed stronger or more determined, and behind whom the others took refuge.

"'Out of my way!' I shouted again, flourishing my cane like a sword.

"'Give up, you dog!' they responded, never once letting up their fantastic dance.

"I no longer had any doubt: they were inebriated. Because they were and because they weren't carrying any arms, I calmed down somewhat. I lowered my cane, and striving to give my words an air of authority, I said:

"'All right, all right. Enough of this foolishness. Let me by now.'

"'Give up, you dog! Are you going to suck the blood of the dead? Are you going to amputate a leg? Tear off somebody's ear? Take out somebody's eye? Pull somebody's nose?'

"This was the outcry that came from the group by way of response to my request. At the same time they advanced closer to me. One of them, not the one who was in front, but another, stretched his arm over the top of the shoulder of the first one and grabbed me by the nose and pulled so hard that I howled in pain. I jumped sideways, because my back was almost touching the wall, and I managed to put some distance between them and me. And raising my cane, blind with rage, I struck the one who was in front. He fell heavily to the floor without uttering 'Oh!' The others fled.

"I was left alone and waited anxiously for the injured man to moan or move. Nothing—not a groan, not even the slightest movement. Then it occurred to me that I could have killed him. The cane really was heavy and all my life I've been obsessed with exercising. With trembling hands I hurriedly pulled out a box of matches and lit one. . . .

"I can't describe to you what went through my mind at that moment. Stretched out on the floor, face up, lay a dead man. Yes, dead! I clearly saw death on his pale face. The match fell from my fingers and once again I was in darkness. I only saw him for an instant but the vision was so intense that not a single detail escaped me. He was obese, had a black, bushy beard and a big, aquiline nose; he was wearing a blue shirt, colored pants, and espadrilles, and on his head was a black boina. He looked like a worker from the arms factory, an armorer, as they usually say there.

"I can assure you, without lying, that the things I thought about in one second, there in the darkness, I wouldn't have time to think about now in an entire day. I saw with perfect clarity what was going to happen: the police arresting me, the consternation of my son-in-law, my daughter fainting, the screams of my granddaughter; then jail, then the trial dragging on interminably for months, maybe years; the difficulty of proving that it had been in self-defense; the district attorney accusing me of being a murderer—the usual procedure in such cases; my defense attorney basing his case on my impeccable background; then the Court's verdict, perhaps absolving me, perhaps condemning me to prison.

"With one jump I reached the street and ran to the corner, but there I realized that I didn't have my hat, and I went back. Once again I entered the hallway with loathing and fear. I lit another match and shot an oblique glance at my victim hoping to see him breathe. Nothing. There he was in the same spot, rigid, jaundiced, not a drop of blood on his face, which made me think that he had died of cerebral shock. I looked for my hat, shoved my fist inside to unwrinkle it, put it on and left.

"But this time I took care not to run. The instinct of self-preservation had taken hold of me completely and suggested all the ways to avoid being apprehended. I hugged the walls in the shadows and, making as little noise as possible, I soon turned the corner at Perseguida Street, entered San Joaquín Street, and headed back to my house. I attempted to appear as calm and composed as possible. But as luck would have it, on Altavilla Street, when I was beginning to settle down, unexpectedly a municipal policeman approached me . . .

"'Don Elías, could you please tell me . . .?'

"I didn't hear another thing. I jumped back so much that I ended up several yards away from the constable. Then, without looking at him, I began a desperate, mad run through the streets to the outskirts of the city, where I stopped, panting and sweating. And I reflected on what I had just done. How stupidly I had behaved! That policeman knew me. He was most likely going to ask me something about my son-in-law. My strange behavior had startled him. He probably thought that I was crazy; but the following morning, when the crime became known, he would become suspicious and inform the judge. My sweat suddenly turned cold.

"I headed home, terrified, and it didn't take me long to get there. On entering I had a clever idea. I went straight to my room, put the iron cane in the closet and took another one that I had, made of rattan, and left again. My daughter, surprised, came to the door. I invented a meeting with a friend at the casino, and, in fact, went there in a hurry. A few of the men who made up the late evening conversation group were still in the room adjacent to the billiard hall. I sat down next to them, I affected good humor, I was excessively jovial and I tried everything imaginable to get them to take notice of the light little cane that I carried in my hand. I bent it until making it into a bow, I flailed my trousers with it, I brandished it like a fencing foil, I touched people on the back with it to ask something, I let it fall to the floor. In short, I left no stone unturned.

"Finally, when the conversation broke up and I took leave of my companions in the street, I was a little more calm. But upon arriving home and being alone in my room, a deadly sadness took hold of me. I understood that that scheme of mine would only serve to aggravate the situation in the event that they came to suspect me. I undressed absent-mindedly and remained seated at the edge of the bed for a long time absorbed in my gloomy thoughts. I finally had to get under the covers because of the cold.

"I was unable to close my eyes. I tossed and turned a thousand times between the sheets, prey of a fatal anxiety, of a terror made more cruel by the silence and solitude. At any moment I expected to hear knocks on the door, footsteps of the police on the staircase. At daybreak, however, I was overcome by sleep— actually a dull lethargy from which I was awakened by the voice of my daughter:

"'It's already ten o'clock, Father. You have rings under your eyes. Did you have a bad night?'

"'On the contrary, I slept like a log,' I hastened to answer.

"I didn't even trust my own daughter. Then I added, affecting naturalness:

"'Has the *Trade Times* already come?'"

"'Yes, of course it has.'"

"'Bring it to me.'

"I waited until she left and spread open the newspaper with trembling hands. I scanned all of it anxiously without seeing anything. Suddenly I read in large type: *THE CRIME ON PERSEGUIDA STREET,* and I froze with terror. I looked more closely. It had been a hallucination. It was an article entitled *THE CRITERION OF THE MEMBERS OF THE PROVINCIAL LEGISLATURE.*

Finally, making a supreme effort to calm down, I managed to read the section of short news items where I found one that said:

STRANGE INCIDENT

The attendants of the Provincial Hospital engage in the reprehensible practice of making use of the peaceful inmates who are in the insane asylum for various tasks, amongst them the transporting of corpses to the autopsy room. Last night four madmen, carrying out this task, found the door that leads to San Ildefonso Park open and fled through it, taking with them the corpse. As soon as the administrator of the hospital was notified of the matter, he dispatched several emissaries in search of them but to no avail. At one o'clock in the morning the four lunatics appeared at the hospital, but without the corpse. It was discovered by the night watchman of Perseguida Street in the hallway of Doña Nieves Menéndez. We implore the senior director of the Provincial Hospital to take measures to ensure that such scandalous occurrences are not repeated.

"I dropped the newspaper and was overcome by convulsive laughter which degenerated into fits of hysterics."
"In other words you had killed a dead man?"
"Exactly."

Alone!

Fresnedo, taking his customary nap, was in a deep sleep. Next to the divan stood the lacquered nightstand smudged with cigar ashes, and on it were a cup and saucer announcing that coffee does not keep everybody awake. The room, furnished for summer use with rockers, cane chairs, and fine straw matting, had bare, frescoed walls, and basked in a half-light that scarcely filtered in through the shutters. For this reason the heat was not felt. For this reason and also because we are in one of the coolest provinces in the north of Spain, and out in the country. Silence prevailed. Outside all that could be heard was the soft snore of cicadas and the peep-peep of a bird who, protected by the tendrils of the gravevine that surrounded the balcony, took pleasure in interrupting the siesta of his companions. Occasionally the squeak of a cart sounded in the distance—a slow, monotonous creak that beckoned one to sleep. Inside the house, the noise of dishes being washed had stopped for some time now. Since she went barefoot, the kitchenmaid—the robust, the colossal Mariona—produced only a slight groan in the floorboards, which complained about supporting such an enormous and massive specimen of humanity.

Anybody would envy the cool room, the delightful silence, the placid sleep. Fresnedo was a sybarite, but only in summertime. During the rest of the year he worked unstintingly in his office on Espoz y Mina Street* where he had a large carpet business. He was in his early forties, strong and healthy as men who did not have a stormy youth usually are; he had dark skin, curly hair, and a long mustache that was beginning to turn gray. Fresnedo was born in Campizos, where we happen to be right now, the son of fairly well-off farmers. His parents sent him to Madrid at the age of fourteen to learn the business from his uncle. He worked with determination and good judgment; he became his uncle's number one clerk, afterwards his associate, and finally he married his daughter, and inherited his property and his business. Fresnedo entered marriage late in life, when he was approaching forty. His wife was only twenty. Brought up in the comforts and even luxury that the old Fresnedo was able to provide for her, Margarita was one of those pampered young Madrid girls, the epitome of finickiness and vanity; she had become a slave to the thousand and one absurdities of capital life as if they were specified by the decrees of some immortal code, and was completely estranged from the life of nature and truth. For that reason she detested the country, and very particularly, the unknown and luxuriant little spot where her humble line had its beginnings. She detested it almost as much as her mama, old Fresnedo's wife, who, in spite of being the daughter of a crockery dealer from Aduana Street, deemed it beneath her to set foot in Campizos.

For as much as the two women detested it, the good Fresnedo loved it. While he was a clerk for his uncle, he obtained permission from him every year to spend the month of July or August in his hometown. When his earnings allowed him to, he erected alongside that of his parents a very pretty little house surrounded by a garden, and began to buy all the plots of land near it that were put up for sale. In not too many years Fresnedo managed to become a respectable proprietor. And as he was becoming the owner of the land where he had spent his early years, his love for it grew disproportionately. Anybody can imagine the displeasure that the honest merchant experienced when, already married to his cousin, she announced to him when summer arrived that she was not "disposed to burying herself in Campizos," a decision which his aunt and recently acquired mother-in-law supported with surprising mettle. It was necessary to resign himself to summering in San Sebastián. The following year the same thing happened. But when the third came, Fresnedo had the audacity to rebel, which caused a great domestic uproar. "Either we go to Campizos or we go nowhere this summer. Do we understand each other, ladies?" And his mustache stood on end in such an inflexible manner when pronouncing these words that his unhappy wife fainted on the spot, and his spirited mother-in-law, sprinkling her daughter's temples with cool water and holding a flask of smelling salts to her nose, began to rebuke him bitterly:

"Smell these, dear, smell these salts. If only things could be done a second time! The fault is mine for having put such a delicate flower in the hands of a brute."

When the delicate flower finally opened her eyes it was to release a torrent of tears and to say in a disconsolate tone:

"I never would have believed it of Ramón!"

Fresnedo was moved. There were explanations. In the end he compromised in honorable fashion for both parties. It was agreed that Margarita and her mama would go to San Sebastián, taking with them their fifteen-month old baby daughter, and that Fresnedo would go to Campizos for the month of August with Jesús, the older child, who was three, and his nursemaid. This is the reason that Fresnedo is taking a nap where we've just seen him.

A well-known voice awakened him from it.

"Papa, Papa."

He opened his eyes and saw his son nearby wearing a pearl-colored drill smock and white shoes; his black, tangled hair was perched on his forehead in amusing curls. The boy was more robust than attractive. His skin, naturally dark-complexioned, had become deeply tanned from the days he had spent living a carefree, almost uncivilized, village life. His father kept him outdoors almost all day long, scrupulously following the doctor's instructions.

"Papa . . . Tata* said that you didn't want . . . that you didn't want . . . to buy me a wagon . . . and that the ram . . . and that the ram wasn't mine . . . that it was Carmita's (his sister), and she won't let me grab it by the horns, and she slapped my hand."

The little boy, on pronouncing this discourse with his tiny tongue, stopping frequently, revealed in his deep, black eyes intense indignation and a great hunger for justice. For a moment it seemed that he was going to break out crying, but his energetic temperament prevailed, and after pausing, he closed his speech with a trooper's swearword. His father had been listening to him enraptured, encouraging him with gestures to continue, as if celestial music were gladdening his ears. On hearing the swearword, he burst into loud and happy laughter. The child looked at him in surprise, unable to understand that what caused him to be beside himself could amuse his papa so much. The latter could have continued listening to him hour after hour without blinking an eye. And yet, as his mother-in-law related to visitors when she wanted to administer the *coup de grâce* to her son-in-law and completely shatter his public esteem, he had fallen asleep listening to Gayarre* sing *La Favorita*.

"Is that so, my love? Tata doesn't want you to grab the ram by his horns? Let me get up. You'll see how I'll straighten her out." Fresnedo drew his son close and gave him two formidable kisses on the cheeks while simultaneously caressing his head with his hands.

The boy had not exhausted the topic of the wrongs that he believed had been inflicted on him by his nursemaid. He continued jabbering that she had refused to give him bread.

"We ate just a little while ago."

"It was a long time ago," the child said defiantly.

"All right, then. I'll give it to you."

Besides, Tata had not wanted to tell him a story nor make him paper cows. Besides, she had pricked him with a pin, here. And he showed his papa his hand.

"You're right!" exclaimed Fresnedo, seeing, in effect, a slight scratch. "Dolores! Dolores!" he shouted afterwards.

The nursemaid appeared. The master upbraided her harshly for keeping pins on her clothing in violation of his express prohibition. Jesús, seeing Tata downtrodden and intimidated, nestled himself against her skirt as if asking pardon for being the cause of her grief.

"All right," Fresnedo said, getting up from the divan and stretching. "Now we'll go to the stable and you'll grab the ram by his horns. Do you want to, Chucho?"*

Chucho attempted to dislocate his head showing signs of the agreement which he confirmed expressively with his tiny tongue. But shooting a timid glance at the same time at his Tata, and seeing her still serious and embarrassed, he said with a disarming smile:

"Don't be angry, silly. You're coming with us too."

Fresnedo put on his drill sack coat, covered his head with a straw hat and, taking his little boy by the hand, went down to the garden, from which point they headed for the stable. On opening the door, Chucho, who had approached with determination, stopped and waited for his father to enter. It was dark. From the rear of the barn came the tepid, moist vapor that livestock always emit. The cows mooed feebly, which put a real scare into

Jesús, who categorically refused to go in under the specious pretext that he was going to soil his shoes. His father then picked him up, went in, and tried to take him close to the cows and have him put his hand on their foreheads. Chucho, who was frightened, confessed that he was "a li'l afraid" of the cows. The rams were something entirely different. He claimed that he could take them or leave them, that he had never felt anything for them except love and veneration.

"All right, let's go see the rams," said his father, smiling.

And they moved to the sheep stalls. Fresnedo attempted to set him down there, but as soon as his feet touched the ground Jesús declared that he was played out, and so he had to be picked up again. His father brought him close to a ram and encouraged him to grasp a horn. It was a serious matter and worthy of consideration. Chucho thought it over carefully. He brought his hand forward tentatively, withdrew it, brought it forward again, and withdrew it again. He finally decided to inform his father that he was "a li'l afraid" of rams. But, on the other hand, he said that he got on famously with chickens, and that never in his life had they frightened him in the slightest, and that he felt confident enough to grab them by the tail, the feet, and even the beak, because they were cowardly, contemptible animals, in his opinion at least. Fresnedo had no objection to taking him to the wire-fence chicken coop which was at the rear of the house. Once there, Chucho, with a display of courage rarely recorded in history, approached the largest rooster, an enormous bird of Spanish stock, haughty carriage, and fiery eye. He tried to grab him by the tail, as he had solemnly promised, but the dignified sultan of the chicken coop screeched in such a horrifying way, flapping his wings and stamping the ground ferociously, that the chill of death penetrated Chucho's heart. He hastened to let him go and clung, terrified, to his father's neck.

"Man, didn't you tell me that you weren't afraid of chickens?" Fresnedo asked, laughing.

"You, you . . . you grab him, Papa."

"I'm afraid."

"No, you're not afraid."

"And are you?"

Ashamed, Jesús stopped talking, but finally he confessed that he was "a li'l afraid" of chickens too.

From there Fresnedo took him back to the stable and, after a few scares and some vacillation, managed to get him to put his hand on a calf's snout. But since it occurred to the animal to stick out his tongue and run it over that same hand, the roughness made such an impression on Chucho that he refused to get close to any other member of the bovine race. Next, Fresnedo took him up to the straw loft. What pleasure for the little boy! Sink in the straw, grab it, scatter it around in small handfuls, and fall backwards with his arms spread open! But even greater was his father's pleasure watching him. They played at burying each other alive. Fresnedo would let himself be covered by his son, who piled straw on him with a vigor and vehemence that nobody would have anticipated. But when it was least expected, his father would shake wildly and the straw would go flying. Each time the boy burst into laughter as if their game were the most amusing thing in the world. Sweat was flowing from every pore of his soft little body, and hair was stuck to his forehead and his face was flushed. When his father tried to take revenge and bury him, Jesús could not bear it. As soon as the straw covered his eyes, he began to scream, and ended up crying in earnest with tears streaming down his cheeks, tears that his father hastened to swallow with passionate kisses.

Yes. At that moment Fresnedo was overcome by one of the fits of tenderness that were frequent in him. Jesús was his whole family, his only love, the sole joy of his life. If we penetrated the innermost recesses of his heart, it's possible that we would not find a whit of affection for his wife. Her haughty, impertinent, and disagreeable character had extinguished the fire of passion that he felt for her on getting married. But that tender shoot, that rosebud, that angelic confection filled his heart and engaged his life completely, and was the substance of his thoughts, the consolation of his sorrows. He embraced him rapturously and covered his rosy cheeks with extended kisses holding him very tightly, murmuring in his ear afterwards the ardent words of a lover:

"Who loves you more than anyone else in the world, my pretty one? Isn't it your papa? Tell me, light of my life. And you, whom do you love the most? Yes, my pet, yes. I love you so much that I would gladly give my life for you. For you, only for you, I would like to be somebody worthwhile in the world. For you, only for you, I work and I will work until I die. I'll never be able to pay you back the happiness you bring me, my son!"

The child did not understand, but he perceived the ardor and repaid it in kind. His big, black, expressive eyes were fixed on his father, and he was struggling to fathom that world of love and decipher the meaning of such fervent words. After a moment of silence in which it seemed that he was meditating, he took his father's face with his little hands that looked like pink carnations and, bringing his mouth close to his ear, said in a voice as soft as a faint breath:

"Papa, I'm going to tell you something . . . I love you more than Mama . . . Don't tell her, all right?"

The good Fresnedo's eyes became moist listening to his son.

They came down from the straw loft and left the stable. After the merchant looked at his watch, he decided to go swimming in the river as he did every day.

"Chucho, are you going swimming with me?"

Heavens above, what joy!

Chucho nearly went mad with happiness. Usually his father's swim caused him to shed a few tears since he could not go along because of the nursemaid. Fresnedo swam in an isolated spot, but stark naked. This time he chose to take his son with him and leave Dolores at home. The boy began to ask in a loud voice for his hat. He did not want to go up inside the house for it fearful that his father would slip away, like other times. Tata, laughing, tossed it to him from the balcony, as well as Fresnedo's sheet and parasol.

The river was a half mile from the house. It was necessary to walk along a number of lanes bordered by uneven, low walls with brambleberry and honeysuckle jutting out of them. The sun was beginning to descend, and the valley, the beautiful valley of Campizos—surrounded by gentle knolls studded with chestnut trees, and in the distance, a stretch of towering mountains whose crests floated in a violent mist—napped silently, displaying its incomparable cloak of verdure. Every shade of green was in this cloak, from the light yellowish of young grass to the dark and deep of oaks and elms.

Father and son walked along the narrow lanes, shading them-selves with the parasol of the latter. But Chucho broke away often and Fresnedo allowed him to run free, convinced that it was good to accustom the boy to the world around him. He delighted in seeing him run ahead wearing his little drill smock and a big straw hat with blue bands. Like dogs, Chucho covered the same distance four times. He stopped frequently to pick flowers that were within his reach, and those that weren't, he despotically obliged his father to pick for him, and to cut, in addition, a few tree branches that he used to sweep the road. In the middle of it he had, to be sure, an unfortunate and frightful encounter. Coming around a bend he ran into a pig—a big, black, stout pig walking in the same direction. Chucho had the temerity to go over to him and grab him by the tail. This accessory of animals exercised a magnetic influence on his diminutive but chubby hands. The pig, who apparently was in a bad humor and jumpy, squealed frightfully on feeling himself seized, and turning around to escape, crashed into the boy and knocked him down. Good Lord, what screams! Fresnedo came on the run, lifted him and wiped away the tears and dust, assuring him that he would take revenge on that barbarous, rude pig when they got home. This placated Chucho, but not without his proclaiming first that the pig was very ugly and that he liked dogs better because they were friendly and knew him and that when they were in the mood they licked his face.

Several times Fresnedo had to jump a hedge or a wall, but first he would take his son in his arms and very carefully set him down on the other side. They left the main road and began to walk through pastureland where Jesús insisted on catching a cricket. His father instructed him to urinate into the hole to drive the insect out. The boy did as he was told, but since the cricket did not want to show, he became upset with himself because he couldn't urinate more, and cried disconsolately. Although with great effort, he gave up that demanding chase and devoted himself to playing *Ladybugs of the Lord*, and entertained himself for a while, too long a while in his father's opinion, placing them in the palm of his hand, singing: *Ladybug, ladybug of the Lord, spread your wings and fly off to the Lord*, a charming little ditty taught to him by Tata, who was well versed in this field of learning.

They finally arrived at the river. It flowed, serene and limpid, among meadows, and was bordered by hazel trees that sprang from the earth like large bouquets. At that spot the river formed a backwater which was known in the village as the Three Waters Pool. It was fairly deep, and the site isolated and inviting. There was no other in the vicinity of Campizos better suited to swimming. The grass came right up to the river's edge, and it was sheer pleasure to sit on that green carpet where anyone could comfortably disrobe without danger of being seen. The hazels, laden with foliage, prevented penetration of the rays of the still bright and blazing sun. Fresnedo enjoyed his swim there more than the sultan of Turkey, storing up health and happiness for the entire year. In that very same spot he had swum as a boy, with a group of friends who were now farmers. What pleasure he experienced remembering particulars of his childhood, when he was a youngster to whom his parents entrusted the care of the livestock on the mountainside or when he helped them with all the farm chores! When remembrances of childhood are associated with an independent life in the bosom of nature, for as poor as one may have been, they always seem happy and delightful.

Father and son rested a few minutes on the grass, relaxing after being in the heat; finally, the former decided to undress. As he slowly removed his clothes, he hummed a song from a musical comedy that he had heard in Madrid. He was overflowing with joy. His son watched him attentively with his big, black eyes. From time to time Fresnedo raised his toward him and said, smiling:

"What's up, Chucho? Do you want to swim with me?"

Chucho was content with laughing, as if to say:

'What a joker you are, Papa! As if you didn't know that I raise a ruckus every time they try to put me in the water!'

Fresnedo swam completely nude. Any kind of bathing suit bothered him a great deal and in that spot he enjoyed the certainty of not being seen. When he was stark naked, the surprise and curiosity written on his Chipilín's* face embarrassed him somewhat, and he covered himself with the sheet. But Chucho didn't fall for it and began to gurgle as he tugged at the sheet with his hands, saying, "that Papa had hair on his body and that he didn't, and that Tata didn't have any either . . ."

"All right, Chucho, that's enough," his papa said to him with a serious expression. "That's not talked about. Children don't talk about that."

"And why don't children talk about that?"

Fresnedo did not answer.

"Why don't children talk about that?" the boy repeated.

The merchant tried to distract him by bringing up something else, but Chucho did not take the bait.

"Why don't children talk about that, Papa?" he insisted, full of curiosity.

"Because it's not good manners," he replied.

"And why isn't it good manners?"

"Enough already, don't pester me!" he exclaimed, half impatient and half smiling.

Wrapped up in the sheet as if he were in a Moorish cape, Fresnedo moved toward the water.

"Listen, Chucho," he said, turning around, "don't move at all. Sit here until I come out, all right? Watch, you're going to see how I go into the water headfirst. Watch me. One . . . two . . . Watch, Chucho . . . three!"

Fresnedo, who had dropped the sheet and stepped onto a small crag while shouting to him, did indeed dive into the pool and he did so with the pleasure of men who enjoy life to the fullest. On making his plunge, his robust body hit the water with such force that it triggered a veritable torrent of a spray that splashed even Jesús. The boy shuddered, astonished and amazed on seeing his father surface quickly and swim, doing somersaults and capers in the water.

"Look, Chucho! Look!"

And he turned belly up, floating without any movement whatsoever on his part.

"Look, look now."

And he swam backwards using only his feet.

"Now you'll see something: I'm going to swim like dogs."

And, sure enough, he swam the dog paddle.

With what exhilaration the wealthy merchant remembered the skills learned in boyhood!

Chucho, entranced, was in utter ecstasy watching him. He did not miss a single one of his movements.

"Chucho! Chunchín! My joy! Who loves you?" shouted Fresnedo, transported by the happiness that the water's caresses and his son's innocent eyes brought to him.

The little boy kept silent, completely absorbed in and attentive to his father's natatorial frolic.

"Come on, tell me, Chipilín. Who loves you?"

"Papa," he replied, serious, his voice slightly hoarse, as he continued watching his father attentively.

One of the skills in which Fresnedo had excelled as a youth and which filled him with much pride was catching trout by hand. Whenever he came to Campizos he practiced this method of fishing. He possessed a truly remarkable ability to explore and batter holes in the rocks, block the trout, and then seize it by the gills. The fishermen of the region acknowledged that he could keep up with any of them; it was said that as a boy he had once come out of the water with three trout, one in each hand and another in his mouth, even though Fresnedo would not confirm the story. In any case, he was suddenly overcome at that moment by the desire to give his son and himself a thrill.

"Now you'll see something, Chipilín. I'm going to bring out a trout for you. Do you want me to?"

You had better believe that he wanted him to!

Especially since it turned out that Chucho felt a greater affinity, if that were possible, for aquatic animals than terrestrial ones!

Fresnedo took a deep breath and plunged downward, leaving his son astonished. He examined the openings of several rocks on the bottom and was only able to touch with his fingers the tail of one trout without managing to grab it. Since he was running out of breath, he came up for air.

"Chucho, I wasn't able to catch it, but it won't give me the slip."

"Why won't it give you the slip?" the child asked, not allowing an idiom to be used without having someone explain it to him.

"What I mean is that I'll catch it."

Again Fresnedo breathed deeply and dove to the bottom. A few moments later he rose to the surface with a trout in his hand, which he tossed to the bank. Chucho squealed with fright and delight upon seeing the little animal at his feet flapping and writhing furiously. The times that it stopped wiggling he attempted to grab it, but on getting his hand close, the trout jumped and a shaken Chucho quickly withdrew it. He would try to grab it again, squealing happily, and another jump would frighten him and cause him to become serious all of a sudden. Chucho was nervous—shouting, laughing, talking, and crying at the same time, while his father, fascinated, swam smoothly and watched him.

"Go ahead, my courageous one! Grab it—it won't do anything to you. By the tail, silly! Do you want me to fish you another one, a bigger one?"

"Yes. Bigger, Papa. I don't like this one," the boy replied, magnanimously refusing to grab such a small trout.

The obliging merchant readied himself for another dive, descended all the way to the bottom, and hurriedly began to probe the holes of a large rock that he had seen earlier. Death, ferocious and treacherous, awaited him inside. He stuck his arm in one that was very narrow, and when he tried to pull it out he couldn't. All his blood rushed to his heart. He panicked trying to determine the way in which it had gone in. He struggled in vain for a few seconds. Finally the hapless Fresnedo opened his mouth, out of breath, and in a matter of seconds was asphyxiated.

Chucho waited in vain for him to come out. For several minutes he looked at the water with intense curiosity until, tired of waiting, he said with innocent naturalness:

"Papa, come out."

His father did not obey him, so he waited a few moments and shouted again, more energetically:

"Papa, come out!"

And more and more impatient, he repeated his shout and ended up crying. For a long time he said again and again in desperation:

"Come out, Papa! Come out!"

His rosy cheeks were awash with tears, and his big, beautiful, innocent eyes were riveted anxiously on the pool, where time after time he imagined seeing his father surface.

A start by the still alive trout, which was nearby, distracted him. He brought his hand close and touched it with a finger. The trout was moving slowly. He touched it again and it moved even less. Then, encouraged by the fish's debility, he ventured to lay the palm of his hand on it. The trout did not stir. Chucho began to mumble softly that he wasn't afraid of trout, and that if his sister Carmina were there she most assuredly would not dare to put her hand on a beast as ferocious as that one. He was becoming so emboldened that he ended up grabbing the fish by the tail and holding it in midair. That act of heroism pleased him so much that sonorous laughter emanated from his throat. But a violent shake from the trout forced him, terrified, to let it go. He glanced about, and not seeing anybody, stared again at the pool and shouted once more while crying:

"Come out, Papa! Come out, Papa! I don't wan' trout, Papa, come out!"

Far off, on the horizon, the sun was going down, hiding behind the tall and distant violet-colored mountains, as that isolated setting, situated on the very slope of the hill, was filling with shadows.

"I' afraid, Papa . . . Come out, Papa!" the distraught youngster continued to shout, swallowing tears.

No voice answered his. The only sounds to be heard were cattle bells or a distant moo. The river continued to murmur softly its eternal lament.

Exhausted and hoarse from so much shouting, Chucho dropped to the grass and dozed off. But his rest was not peaceful. He was an excessively nervous child, and the agitated state in which he had fallen asleep caused him to awaken shortly afterwards. Night had fallen. At first he did not realize where he was and said, like other times in his bed:

"Tata, I want a drink."

But seeing that Tata was not responding, he sat up on the grass and looked around. His little heart cringed in terror when he perceived that he was enveloped by darkness.

"Tata, Tata!" he shouted repeatedly. Moonlight shimmered on the water. With his eyes drawn to the tremulous gleam, he suddenly remembered that his papa was with him and that he had plunged into the river to catch him a trout. And amidst sobs that were breaking his heart and tears that were blinding him, he resumed shouting:

"Come out, Papa. Come out, my papa! I' afraid!"

The child's voice echoed sorrowfully in the silent country darkness. Oh! If the loving Fresnedo could have heard him at the bottom of the well, he would have chewed at the rock that held him fast, he would have wrested his arm from it to respond to his son's call.

Unable to shout any longer because he was out of both voice and breath, and overcome with fatigue, Jesús fell asleep again, which was how he was found by those who had gone in search of him and his papa.

Seduction

The editor of a certain literary journal had asked me for a story for his new publication. I said to him what's usually said in these situations: that I was very honored, that I'd be most happy to write it as soon as my affairs permitted, that surely it wouldn't meet his expectations, et cetera, etc. In short, what we all say to respond graciously to the request of a nice, likeable person. All well and good, but the editor didn't believe me. I could see it in his eyes. And since he didn't believe me, he didn't stop insisting, in spite of my promise, endeavoring to make my word lose the pleasant vagueness that it had for me and assume an awful, unpleasant precision.

"Will you give it to me for the next issue? When, approximately, will I be able to pick it up? May I announce it as of now on the cover?"

I answered each of these queries in the most absurd and ambiguous manner that you can imagine, always defending that precious vagueness with all of my strength. The editor believed me, or affected believing me, and left my house satisfied, so it seemed.

But he wasn't. I became convinced of it when, a few days later, I saw him enter the English Pub, sit down next to me, and drink coffee reluctantly. He talked about inconsequential matters, was amiable and friendly, and didn't mention at all the dreadful promise. He touched on the subject of my novels and said lovely things about them, which proved to me that that man of letters understood well the hearts of his companions. But what he singled out for praise was my collection of short pieces entitled Etchings.* I confess that the nicer he was the more disheartened I became. "Hang it all!"—I said to myself'—. "After this, how would I have the nerve to refuse him the story?" When he said good-bye, I stayed, meditating a little while; I ate the last lump of sugar, drank the last swallow of water, and said, sighing: "Well, sir, the only thing I can do is write an *etching*."

I immediately set about searching for the plot. I left the pub with that sole aim and headed for the street to see if out in the open one would come to the aid of my lonely thoughts. The heat of a pub is disastrous for plots: I draw this fact to the attention of young naturalist writers. Almost as disastrous as the poetry soirées at the Athenaeum. I was informed of this by a dramatic poet who had a play booed not long ago at the Spanish Theater, and he blamed his failure on the dense atmosphere that he breathed in the afternoons and on too many lectures. So ever since, when I need ideas, I desert the Athenaeum and go as fast as I can to the Moncloa, a place where, according to my friend, great thoughts usually occur to a person. The only applauded quatrains of his failed play were composed there.

I left, then, as I've said, and in short and unsteady steps, the usual gait of one who has to say something in a literary journal and doesn't know what to say, I walked up San Jerónimo Avenue to the Puerta del Sol, and from there, along Arenal Street, towards the above mentioned Moncloa Boulevard, hoping that before I arrived at the latter, and only because of the good intentions that I evinced, fortune would furnish me with a reasonably agreeable little storyline.

Almost everybody knows what it's like to be stamped on the corns, but only writers in the public eye know what it's like to search for a plot. If, my reader, you're a hunter, you'll be able to picture something similar by recalling one of those days when one walks for hours and hours through thickets of rockrose under a brutal sun, without glimpsing a single flock of partridges or the small gray head of a rabbit. And imagining the disconsolate, melancholy, and engrossed expression on your face at such moments, you'll be able to figure out what that of yours truly was like while tramping the streets of Madrid.

"Hello, Vinagrera, how are you?"

"Forgive me, my friend. The name's Vinajeras, not Vinagrera."

"Excuse me, for heaven's sake. I got confused right now . . ."

"There's nothing unusual about that. You writers have so much subject matter running through your minds!"

"True, true," I replied brazenly, instead of extending my hand and saying like beggars: 'Give me one plot, for the love of God.'

A little further on I very smilingly said hello to a person who looked at me with astonishment and didn't return my greeting.

"What can I be thinking of?" I asked myself, blushing. I imagined that I was on speaking terms with that gentleman when I only knew him from seeing him standing opposite my house making faces at the woman on the third floor.

On passing in front of the Royal Theater I was suddenly inspired to write a story based on a certain incident in which figured a ballerina whom I had the honor of seeing for a short time. But it was going to turn out a little risqué, and ever since my bookseller friend Mr. Fe told me that my writings are finding favor among the ladies, I've been so intimidated and fearful that I scarcely dare mention a shirt or shorts by name so as not to offend them. At Oriente Square I saw looking out, from the uppermost balconies of the Royal Palace, a young couple who were laughing and talking, while a flock of birds flew around them, alighting on cornices to listen to their tender words, and flying off afterwards with shrill cries to pass them on to their companions. One of the sentries who guard the entrances to the square, motionless astride his horse, was staring at the smitten couple. And God only knows the mad thoughts that his brilliant Prussian-style helmet must have been concealing at that moment! It occurred to me then that I could write a tale situating the action on the upper floors of the Palace, one that could just as easily be about men as about birds. But I immediately took into account that those of my political persuasion are very suspicious. They were sure to see in this story an indirect, underhand means of approaching the Monarchy and betraying our ideals. If because of it I were made a minister or even something of a controversial nature, I know full well that they wouldn't say anything to me. Others have done it without angering them. But to speak of palaces without hatred and without having received any favors at all from them, this isn't logical. No good extremist has ever tolerated such a thing, nor ever will.

I continued uphill to the Argüelles district, opened the gate to the Agricultural Institute, and paused a moment to contemplate the scenery. The area west of Madrid is of such an austerity, presents such an impressive appearance to the eye, that it has always moved me. Only philistines persist in denying beauty to this piece of black, harsh land that is cut off in the distance by the snow-covered Guadarrama. Most people admire no more than what has been admired before by others: the gulf of Naples, the great canal of Venice, the lake at Geneva, Mont Blanc, and Mount Cenis. Besides, to see these sights you have to take a costly trip, have a good position. And everybody knows how much the cost of a trip influences the beauty of the countryside. Although penniless, I'm a broad-minded soul and admire the Guadarrama mountain range. At that hour it projected a bluish cast, and its black flanks sliced through the white shroud of snow with which winter had dressed it. Some long, thin, violet clouds, shaped like eyebrows, hung suspended over it, standing out against a milky sky. The sun, enveloped in a mass of fiery vapors, observed it arrogantly before dipping below the horizon. It has never deigned to pay the Guadarrama a visit, and from the time that it rises until the time that it sets, is content to look at the mountain. The land that stretches out before the latter is poor, useless for livestock; there are no fields of wheat and barley, no merry green meadows. For the greater part it's covered with rockrose and broom, and dotted all over with strawberry trees. The dark green vegetation, the huge rocks with monstrous shapes scattered around the ground since the great geological cataclysms, and the severe lines of its uneven ridges, give this scenery a tragic, distressing, somber appearance that vividly impresses the spirit. But, alas, its strange beauty will never enjoy a good reputation because neither men of good position nor livestock are admirers of what's tragic.

I walked for a while through the fields of the School of Agriculture, and went down, finally, to the old gardens on royal property. There were more soldiers and petticoat cooks than writers in the public eye. It didn't surprise me. Not too many of them are in yet on the secret of my friend the dramatic poet. Relying on his experience and my own, I began a slow stroll along the winding paths, and so that my mind might be more accessible to the good ideas that are concealed there in the tops of the trees, I removed my hat and walked with it in my hand, at the risk of catching a cold. But either they were asleep or they had no desire to change position, because they didn't stir, in spite of the fact that never in my life did I summon them with greater necessity. I imagine that they were frightened off by the dreadful blasts of some recruits to whom a corporal was teaching the basics of the art of playing the bugle.

At the end of a long half hour of walking back and forth, I

observed with pleasure that my head was beginning to swell up, and I heard something rattling around inside it, like when chickpeas fall to the floor. It's a wonderful sign, according to my friend. There never occurred to him one of those scenes that cause audiences to erupt in *Bravos*, and are printed in the newspapers the following day, without his first hearing the familiar chickpeas in his head.

I got ready to receive the inspiration with the greatest concentration possible and in a comfortable position. I sat on a stone bench. Behind me I heard the buzz of a conversation and was tempted to get up; but when I turned around, I noticed that it was a young couple chatting with their backs to me and sitting on another bench no softer than mine. I took a real fancy to half of that couple at first glance. Not the other half. And in consideration of the first, I decided to wait a moment, without bearing in mind that you can't play around with inspiration.

The latter (not the inspiration, the first half of the couple) was a round-faced plump, young woman with bright, expressive eyes and a slightly upturned nose. Not a handsome thing, but certainly very animated. The gentleman at her side was neither handsome nor animated. He was skinny, had a very long face with prominent cheekbones, and a full, unkempt, blond beard; his eyes appeared lifeless and dull—the very picture of languor and sluggishness. Some reader will say, reading this description: "What searching observations these realist writers make! This one describes chapter and verse the faces of those two young people, and their backs were turned to him." If you say this without irony, dear reader, many thanks; but if you've learned humorous refinements at the Lara Theater and speak with a veiled meaning, I'll point out that their backs were turned, true, but at an oblique angle to me. The result was that in the normal sitting position I saw half of their faces, and when, on gesticulating, they changed posture, I saw the whole face. There's more (and forgive the presumption): I believe that she showed me hers on purpose when she noticed, and she noticed it rather quickly, that she didn't displease me by doing so. "Oh, women!" exclaimed my friend the dramatic poet when I told him about it, and he ended up immersed in a sea of deep, doleful reflections, which I didn't dare to interrupt.

My aptitude for observation prompted me to grasp quickly that they were married, aided somewhat by these words I distinctly overheard the female half say:

"Since we've been married you haven't ordered any shirts, have you?"

Ugh! Shirts! Forgive me, ladies, forgive me! I've let this indecent word slip out. It won't happen again.

The married couple's conversation was most prosaic. Nevertheless, the young wife seemed more and more poetic to me. I don't know what it is about pretty women, who even when they mention sh . . . . gently touch the heart. She discussed linens with the competence of a washerwoman, enveloping her husband in such a tender, passionate glance that it really was enough to drive him mad. This didn't prevent her from doing what she could in passing to drive me mad, occasionally directing towards my bench swift, provocative peeks that were little by little making this humble writer go soft in the head, rendering it useless for the moment to write a story intended for *Modern Spain* or any other publication. The fact of the matter is that I didn't remember my commitment at all. The young wife knew it perfectly well, I'm certain, and encouraged me to persevere in forgetting through an endless series of demure gestures fraught with coquetry, which undoubtedly were intended to bewitch me or make me succumb with admiration. The cute and adorable things that that young temptress did in a short time with her eyes, with her lips, with her hands, and, in general, with all of her plump person, cannot be described.

But at the same time that I felt attracted and captivated by her charms, pangs of remorse were taking possession of my soul. As for morality, I don't consider myself a hero out of Pérez Escrich* or out of the *Children's Reader*, but I don't take it personally either when I hear preachers talk about "these depraved, abject beings wallowing in vice." I profess as much respect for marriage as, at the least, a conservative member of parliament. I know full well, because I've read it in Krause's *Ideal of Humanity*, with notes by Sanz del Río,* that "men and women in all their individuality should join together to create an indissoluble bond and reconcile the basic and the most deep-rooted point of resistance in our nature, that of sex, by forming a superior being for the joint fulfillment of all human ends." It was, therefore, logical that

the pleasure afforded me by contemplation of the charming wife
and the exchange of glances, which had become established
between us, be accompanied by a bitter aftertaste. Violation of
the precepts of morality always produces it. The young
woman's rosy cheeks seduced me; her fresh, moist mouth
triggered in me the gentlest quiver, either in my body or my
spirit, I'm not certain which. But at the same time, the thought
that through my fault those young people wouldn't reconcile
the basic and most deep-rooted point of resistance in our
nature, and wouldn't achieve the joint fulfillment of its ends,
infused me with horror and sadness.

I had half a mind to get up and move away from that spot,
thereby satisfying my conscience. I beg the reader to believe me.
Just as I was going to carry out this praiseworthy thought, which
heaven will surely reward, I know not in what form, I observed
that the couple had changed their topic of conversation. They
were no longer discussing underwear, but something even more
intimate: the girlfriends that the husband had had before
marrying. They lowered their volume, but I still heard them reasonably well, especially him, because he had a gruff voice, the
kind in which a falsetto would be an impossibility. Furtively I
slid along the bench until I reached the end of it.

"But which of the two did you love more—Felisa or Socorro?"
she was asking.

"Neither. The only one I loved, and you already know it, is
María."

"Yes, yes," she rejoined in a melancholy tone. "I know that you
loved her more than me."

"Don't be silly. More than you, nobody. María was a nice girl,
very plain, very affectionate . . ."

"Naturally! For that very reason! Because she was more worthy
than me you loved her more."

"I didn't say that she was more worthy than you. She was nice,
and you are too . . . , and I loved you more since I married you."

She was silent and downcast for a few moments, as if she
doubted her husband's words, and the doubt caused her grief.
Finally, raising her cute little head and looking at him with mischievous eyes, and then glancing at me with even more mischievous eyes, she ventured to ask him timidly:

"And you've never had an affair with a married woman?"

"No, never," he replied, while drawing lines in the sand with his walking stick.

"Come on, don't be a hypocrite, Lonchín! All you men like forbidden fruit."

And as she was saying this she was giving me a teasing, smiling glance that electrified me.

Lonchín persisted in his denial, continuing to draw geometric designs in the sand.

"Really, Lonchín, tell me about it . . . It doesn't matter, so I won't get angry . . . Provided that from now on you're faithful to me . . ."

"I'm telling you that I didn't. Making a fool of another man or robbing him of his happiness has always seemed like a contemptible act to me."

It's clear that Lonchín had also read Krause's *Ideal of Humanity*, and to greater advantage.

They were silent for a few moments. Finally, the husband let out a little nasal chuckle, making at the same time a pretty border with his walking stick. He seemed to be laughing at his own thoughts, at some recollection that had suddenly crossed his mind.

"I knew it! You've done something forbidden!" the wife exclaimed, half smiling, half angry.

"No, my love, and I'm going to tell you what did happen so you won't imagine all sorts of disparate things. Pay attention for a bit. It was around January of the last year of my studies, and in June I would graduate as an engineer. One Saturday I received at my lodgings a card from Moreno, my agent, whom you know, telling me that that evening he couldn't go to the Comedia, where he had a season ticket, and that if I wanted to, I could use his box seat—row seven, number five—by presenting the card to the usher. It really excited me because I usually went to the theater on Saturdays, but it was to the upper gallery of the Royal where you get soaking wet with perspiration. The prospect of enjoying a box seat in a good theater without it costing me a cent enticed me. I got all dressed up, as elegantly as I could, and after having coffee with my friends, I went to the Comedia. In the row behind me, that is, in eight, there was an attractive woman, plump and a little snub nosed, just like you. Of course you know that I don't care for any other type of woman. Bewitching eyes, the kind that really arouses a man's curiosity . . . , like yours."

"Thanks very much."

"You're welcome."

"Next to her was a young and not bad-looking gentleman who must've been her husband. Well, since I don't smoke and had few friends at that time, instead of going out to the foyer I devoted myself to watching that woman, who, I confess to you, enthralled me. Apparently her husband was unaffected and not very jealous. He didn't take much notice of it, in spite of the fact that my eyes were glued to her. He read newspapers, the *Post*, the *Courier*, the *Herald*, one each between acts. On the other hand, she noticed it admirably fast, and in truth, I don't think it displeased her. In any case, with a certain slyness she would cast occasional glances at me, inflating my ego beyond description. That crossfire of quick looks lasted all evening. I wasn't paying much attention at all to the performance; I was nervous, yet delighted. I'd never been in a more awkward situation. I don't know what pipe dreams I was concocting for the future!

"When the performance ended, I managed to exit alongside her and had the pleasure of feeling the sweet pressure of her arm against mine. I was afraid she'd leave in a carriage. Fortunately that didn't happen. They headed for home on foot, arm in arm, which I considered a personal affront. In my view, no man any longer had the right to give his arm to that woman except me. They continued on to the end of Príncipe Street, escorted closely by yours truly, followed Huertas to Matute Square, then took Atocha Street to Santa Isabel. Every now and then, with little attempt to conceal it now, she would turn around. With each glimpse I felt myself transported to seventh heaven. Finally, they started up Salitre Street. It was quite dark and completely deserted at that hour. All of a sudden, I saw my beautiful femme fatale turn around with even more boldness than before, and after ascertaining that I was but a short distance away, she stood on tiptoe, got her husband's attention as if she were going to say something in his ear, and planted on his cheek the loudest, noisiest kiss I've ever heard . . . I nearly fainted from shame and indignation."

"Marvelous!" exclaimed the young woman, laughing gaily. And then, tossing me a quick glance, she said:

"Listen, Lonchín, that kiss—was it as good as this one?"

Saying and doing, she bent towards him and planted a kiss on his lips that, to tell the truth, could stand comparison with any one.

I gave a start and crept away from there.

Full of spite?

No. Happy, because I had my storyline in my head.

Clotilde's Romance

Every night up to a half dozen male admirers meet in Clotilde's dressing room; Clotilde is the leading lady in one of the capital's most important theaters. The gathering almost always lasts as long as the performance, but it is interrupted now and then. When the actress needs to change her costume, she turns to the group with a graceful smile and supplicating eyes:

"Gentlemen, will you excuse me for a moment? Just for a moment."

They all adjourn to the lounge and wait patiently. I'm mistaken, not all, because the youngest of them, who's been studying for three years to become an M.D., takes advantage of the opportunity and leaves to stroll through the wings to stretch his legs a little and snatch a misdirected kiss. In any event, the majority pace back and forth or sit, waiting for Clotilde to open the door halfway and stick out her queen's or peasant's head, depending on the role she's going to play, and call out to them:

"Come in, gentlemen. Did I take long?"

For Don Jerónimo, it's always long. He's the last one to leave, grumbling all the while, and the first one to go back inside her room. He is not altogether reconciled to this chaste habit. And although he may not dare to voice his feelings, in the back of his mind he considers it an imposition to have to absent himself so that this babe in arms can get dressed—he, who has spent thirty years of his life behind the scenes and has been a close friend of all retired and present actors and actresses.

Don Jerónimo is fifty-four years old and has worked in the Overseas Ministry since the age of twenty-five. Every new government has respected him as an indispensable wheel in the administrative machinery of the colonies. A bachelor and martyr for landladies. It's said that back in his younger days he wrote a play that earned him catcalls and a lifelong entrée into the theatrical world. Resigned or not resigned to the audience's assessment, he stopped writing plays and assumed the noble role of patron of unknown authors and artists as well as insolvent companies. The young man who came to Madrid from the provinces with a play under his arm could set out on no better path to see it performed than the one leading to Don Jerónimo's house. He received everything with open arms, good and bad. Nevertheless, since he possessed very rough manners he didn't spare the novices who trusted in him and read him their plays strong criticism and even insults: "That whole speech is pure hodgepodge. Get rid of it." "Now listen here, you innocent creature. How do you expect a man who's about to kill another to reel off seventeen ten-line stanzas without a break?" "Good Lord, what rubbish! Platonic love for a prostitute! You're wet behind the ears, young man!" Whoever caught a little of his drift didn't become upset, kept going, and at the conclusion of the reading placed the manuscript in Don Jerónimo's hands. And it was quite certain to be staged. The old theater hand exercised considerable influence interlaced with fear over management and actors, and when he got vexed, he had a sharp tongue. If the play was booed, he would protest in a fit of anger against the audience's judgment and continue to patronize the playwright even more persistently. If the play was a big success, he would keep quiet and smile with gratification, but he wouldn't back the acclaimed poet again. When the latter complained of his indifference, Don Jerónimo would respond: "You've already taken wing; so, fly away, my friend, fly away, because I have to set other poor things free."

There was nothing very unusual about his private life. Every night on leaving the theater he went to the Habanero café where he invariably dined on steak accompanied by a small beer. According to a certain friend who had observed him time after time, he always arranged his evening repast so skillfully that he would simultaneously finish the last mouthful of meat, the last piece of bread, and the last sip of beer.

The gathering appears very animated tonight. The actress's friends are chatting and laughing more than usual. Don Jerónimo, wrapped up in his cape (it's a concession), settled comfortably in the corner chair and with an habitual cigar in his mouth (also a concession), tells terrific jokes that occasionally cause the listeners to glance towards Clotilde and which make the latter's cheeks blush slightly. Don Jerónimo doesn't notice this; he's known her for so long that he thinks he has the right to disregard certain courtesies shown to ladies, assuming that he's shown them to any woman in his life, which we doubt. At the time that he met her Clotilde was very young, living meagerly and learning the dressmaker's trade; it was Don Jerónimo who steered her to the theater. Today, thanks to her talent, she earns enough to support her mother and her sisters with dignity.

Clotilde, graceful and pleasant more than beautiful, has a dark complexion and almond-shaped black eyes, the prettiest feature of her face; her mouth is somewhat big, but fresh, and she possesses an admirable set of teeth. She's dressed as a gentlewoman of the time of Louis XV with a white wig that looks marvelous on her. She scarcely takes part in the conversation. She seems satisfied just to listen, continuously turning her serene eyes from one speaker to another and smiling often when they address her.

On arriving at a certain point, the callboy's voice is heard:

"Miss Clotilde, whenever you're ready."

"Let's go on," she says, standing up.

She heads for the mirror, applies the final touches to her eyebrows and eyelashes with the brush, and arranges with slightly nervous hands the curls of the wig, the diamond cross round her neck, and the pleats of her dress. Her admirers keep silent for a moment and casually contemplate these operations.

"Gentlemen, see you later."

And she leaves the room followed by her maid, who carries the gathered-up train, a magnificent cream-colored satin train.

"This Clotilde is getting prettier by the day," says the medical student, letting out an imperceptible sigh.

Don Jerónimo takes an enormous puff on his cigar and is instantly enveloped in a cloud of smoke. Therefore nobody notices the smile of the triumph with which he receives the observation.

"She seems prettier by the day to me too," says another member of the group, "but I believe her disposition's been modified considerably for some time now. You, young man, didn't know her as we did. She was a charming, crazy little thing—so happy, so lively! Nobody could be at her side in a bad humor. Now I find her serious, almost sad . . ."

"It's true that I've been surprised by the melancholy in her eyes."

Don Jerónimo took another enormous puff on his cigar. Nobody saw the flash of anger that streaked across his face.

"These changes, young man, are only brought about by love."

"Some boyfriend?"

"It's . . . it's a story Don Jerónimo knows well."

"I'll tell it," the old theater hand said in a muffled voice that came from inside his cape, "and believe me, talking about childish selfishness is not a palatable prospect, but the story has to do with a young woman whom we all love, and whatever affects her should interest us.

"Around three years ago an elegantly dressed young man with the manuscript of a play under his arm approached the director of this theater. Nothing in this world is more imposing and frightening than a well-dressed young man who's carrying under his arm the manuscript of a play. The director tried to duck out of it, made a few artful dodges and several feints, but in the end he was beaten at his own game; I mean that one day the young man invited him to lunch, enticed him by presenting the prospect of several dozen oysters marinated in Sauternes, and for dessert dumped the play in his lap.

"It turned out to be a real *bomb*. Pepe did, as you all know, what's usually done in cases of this sort: he was deeply impressed with the versification, said 'Bravo' on arriving at certain complicated thoughts, and, lastly, suggested some minor revisions in the second act, which would make the piece just right.

"The gullible poet went home very pleased and set to work eagerly on the revisions. A fortnight later he showed up again, but then Pepe found the first act a little languid and advised him to give it at all costs more action and to shorten it somewhat. It took the poet a month to rewrite the first act. When he came back, the director, always appearing most impressed with the versification and a few of the ideas, expressed some doubts that the work was indeed *theatrical*. He had none that it was *literary*; on the contrary, it seemed to him that in this regard it could compete with the best works of Ayala* . . . ; but theatrical, really theatrical . . . now that was another matter."

"What's the difference, Don Jerónimo? I don't understand."

"Well I'll explain it to you, young man. Behind the scenes we call the good plays theatrical, and the bad ones literary."

"Oh!"

"After expressing these doubts, he ended up suggesting a number of other minor revisions in the third act.

"The poet finally understood; a truly marvelous thing, because poets, who comprehend everything, who know why the condor flies so high, who rise to the heavens and plunge to abysses and penetrate the inner meaning of all created things, are not capable of understanding that at times their works don't meet with the approval of those who listen to them. Our young man, whom we'll call Inocencio, picked up his manuscript a little peevishly and went some time without putting in an appearance; but finally, no doubt after having meditated profoundly, he showed up one morning at Clotilde's house. I don't have to tell you that he was carrying the manuscript under his arm.

"He waited patiently in the drawing room for our actress to complete her *toilette*, and when at length she appeared, Clotilde saw in front of her a confused and blushing but pleasant and elegant young man who begged her with stammering speech to grant him the favor of listening to the reading of a play. All of you must know that women very much like wielding the power of a patron, most especially on behalf of pleasant, elegant young men. Therefore it will not surprise you that Clotilde listened patiently to the play and even found it acceptable. The young man entrusted himself to her completely, depositing the manuscript in her beautiful hands as if it were a recently born baby, and she picked it up like a loving mother and took it under her protection, promising to watch over its precious existence and introduce it to the world. The young man declared that such resolve was worthy of the noble heart whose reputation had already reached his ears. Clotilde responded that it wasn't kindness on her part to support the staging of his play, but an act of justice. The young man said that he was immensely gratified by that idea because Clotilde's exceptional talent and the soundness of her judgment were well-recognized by all, but he didn't dare to indulge in such wishful thinking. Clotilde declared that there were many undeserved reputations in the world and that one of them was hers, but that on this occasion she thought she was in the right. The young man rejoined that where there's smoke there's fire, and that when everybody insists on admiring not only a person's singular beauty and artistic inspiration, but also the evident talent and sparkling erudition, it was necessary to bow one's head. Clotilde said that she would not do so on this occasion because she was quite persuaded that people were very mistaken with regard to what they called her talent and that it was nothing more than pure instinct. The young man raised a storm of protest against this distortion which had absolutely no basis in fact, but suddenly becoming mollified, he was deeply touched in the face of his patron's modesty and swore by all the saints in heaven that never had he met anyone like her. In short, in our kind friend's heart the manuscript was gaining ground by the minute, and the young man took leave of her, overcome with emotion, until the following day.

"The following day Clotilde approached the impresario and extracted from him, by threatening to cancel her contract, a promise to mount a production of Inocencio's play as soon as possible. The young man expressed his gratitude to his patron that very afternoon, and in addition made her his confidante. He belonged to a prominent provincial family, although not one especially well-off. He had come to Madrid to try his luck, trusting solely in his creative ability. In his hometown people said that he had talent and that if he published in Madrid the verses that he had inserted in the *Tagus Herald* he would be compared with Núñez de Arce and Grilo.* He didn't know if this was true, but he had a heart full of noble intentions and loved the theater more than anything else in the world. Would he become an Ayala or a Tamayo?* Would he be rejected by the theater-going public? It was an impenetrable mystery for him.

"At this meeting Clotilde learned two extremely important facts, namely, that Inocencio was bursting at the seams with talent, and that there was nobody in Madrid who tied a cravat with more style. I don't have to tell you that the confidential meetings occurred frequently, and as a result of them, that Clotilde every day suffered the fascinating influence of this supernatural cravat. At last she admitted defeat, surrendering to it unconditionally. The cravat condescended to raise her from the floor and grant her the favor of his affection."

"What do you mean, the cravat?" asked someone who was dozing.

Don Jerónimo took a huge, infernal puff on his cigar as a sign of his displeasure, and proceeded, ignoring the question.

"Around that time rehearsals began for Inocencio's play, which was titled, if memory serves me, *To Go up Going down*; wait, wait, I think it was the reverse, *To Go down Going up* . . . Well, in any event, it was an infinitive and a gerund. I observed immediately that our actress friend and the playwright had started seeing each other; and since, for as bad a poet as Inocencio was—according to what Pepe told me—he really did seem like an honorable young man, I was glad that they had and encouraged them however I could. Clotilde opened up to me, declaring that she was hopelessly in love; that her aspirations no longer had anything to do with the stage, which struck her as an unbearable servitude; that her ideal consisted of living quietly, even if it were in an attic, married to the man whom she adored; that woman had been born to be the guardian angel of the home and not to amuse an audience; and that she placed greater value on reigning over a humble abode illuminated by love than on all the applause on earth. In a word, gentlemen, our friend was head over heels in love.

"Inocencio was no less in love, so it seemed. I bumped into them often strolling through the secluded sections of Retiro Park, at a respectable distance from Clotilde's mama, who would stop opportunely to gaze at the early flower buds or some curious insect. Mamas, in this period of pre-marital crisis, are under obligation to be admirers of nature. The lovebirds would stop on seeing me and greet me with blushing faces. I can't conceal from you that although I regretted it for the theater, I was glad that Clotilde would be getting married. A woman always needs a man's support. And the fact is that they were worthy of each other physically: Inocencio had a very attractive presence.

"At the theater they talked about nothing else except this marriage in infancy. Everybody was glad because Clotilde is the only artist, since the beginnings of time, to have achieved success in the difficult undertaking, until now considered unsurmountable, of winning the affection of her sister actresses.

"I observed, nevertheless . . . All of you know that I'm observant; it's the only quality that I possess, observation, to which playwrights pay no attention now. Today everything in plays is rubbish, a lot of moonbeams that break up as they pass through the foliage of trees, a lot of description of dawn and dusk, a lot of involved similes . . . That's what it all is! When some green playwright comes to me with such nonsense, I say to him: to the point, get to the point! The point is the play, which doesn't exist in the majority of the above."

"Are you getting angry, Don Jerónimo?"

"Well, as I was telling you, I observed that, as the rehearsals progressed, Inocencio's ascendancy over our friend increased. The tone in which he spoke to her was no longer the humble and courtly one of the beginning: now he often corrected her elocution, showed her the attitudes and gestures that she ought to adopt, and sometimes, when the actress didn't fully comprehend his wishes, he reached the point of speaking harshly to her in public and looking at her even more harshly. Our poet ranted and raved like a lord and master. Clotilde accepted it willingly. She, who was so scornful of the most renowned playwrights, now became pliable and moldable like soft wax in the hands of this insipid popinjay. You ought to have seen the humility with which she accepted his corrections and the anxiety that his reproaches caused her. While the rehearsal lasted she didn't take her eyes off him, keeping a watch, like a submissive slave, on her master's desires. The poet, settled comfortably in an armchair with the brazier in front of him, directed the production in the dictatorial manner that García Gutiérrez* or Ayala could have done it. One glance from him sufficed to make Clotilde blush or turn pale. The others didn't protest out of respect for her. When she left the stage she would quickly go and sit next to her fiancé, who sometimes deigned to welcome her with a regal smile, other times with an Olympian indifference. I was scandalized.

"Once I went up close behind them and listened to what they were saying. Clotilde was doing the talking, maintaining fervently that Inocencio's *To Go up Going down* or *To Go down Going up* was better than *A New Drama.** The young man resisted feebly. Another time she spoke about their future marriage. Clotilde described enthusiastically the secluded spot where they would go to keep their happiness a secret; an upper floor in the Salamanca district, flooded with light, a smiling baby, a retreat where Inocencio would work in his study, writing plays, while she would embroider at his side in the strictest silence. When he tired they'd chat for a moment to rest, and afterwards she'd give him a kiss and he'd resume his work. They'd go out, arm in arm, in the evening to take a stroll and then return home. No theater; she detested it with all her heart. In the spring they'd go for walks in the Retiro during the morning and have their chocolate under the trees; and in the summer, spend a month or two in Inocencio's home province, to stock up in the country on good color and health for the winter.

"The description of this tender idyll, which made my heart— even though I'm getting on in years—dance with joy, produced in the playwright nothing more than an impertinent somnolence that only vanished abruptly when he gave, in an imperious voice, some instructions to the actors.

"The day of the premiere finally arrived. We were all anxious to see the result. The general view was that the play had little going for it, but since Clotilde had put her heart and soul in the role it was expected to be a big success. In the dress rehearsal our friend had worked real wonders. There was a moment in which the few of us who attended it as spectators stood up electrified, beside ourselves, shouting at the top of our voices. You can't imagine how splendidly she spoke her part. It was then that an idea suddenly came into my head. Tying up loose ends on my observations of Clotilde's romance I became utterly convinced that Inocencio, on getting her to fall in love with him, had set out only to secure an exceptional interpretation of the protagonist's role in his play and thus assure himself gratifying success. I declined to communicate my suspicions to anyone. I remained silent and waited, but naturally from that point on I found him disagreeable.

"The fuss that Inocencio's friends had made over the play, Clotilde's having chosen it for his benefit, and the widespread belief that in it the celebrated actress was going to achieve a stunning triumph, made it easy for the scalpers to resell all the tickets at exorbitant prices. I know a marquis who paid eleven *duros* for two orchestra seats. The room that we're in now filled up, like every year, with flowers and trinkets; you couldn't walk in the midst of so many porcelain knickknacks, beautifully bound books, ebony jewelry cases, picture frames, and no end of miscellaneous articles.

"The theater was aglitter. Blue-blooded ladies; illustrious politicians, literati, and bankers; the *high life*,* as the saying goes now. But even more aglitter and radiant was Inocencio; radiant with happiness and glory, graciously receiving all the visitors who came to see the gifts, giving orders to the callboys and stagehands for the proper stage scenery and multiplying his smiles and handshakes ad infinitum. Clotilde, likewise, appeared more lovely than ever, her expressive face betraying the sweet emotion that engulfed her and the longing to win laurels for her beloved.

"The curtain rose and everybody went to take his seat. Only five or six of us friends stayed in the wings with the playwright. The opening scenes were, as usual, received indifferently; the following ones, with some signs of approval. The versification was smooth and polished, and the audience, as you all know, takes a liking to catchy expressions. The moment arrived for Clotilde to make her entrance on stage, and there was a ripple of curiosity and expectation. She spoke her part carefully, but without much ardor: you could tell that she was gripped by fear. The curtain went down in silence.

"The lounge and promenades filled instantly with Inocencio's friends, who were quick to tell him that the exposition of his play was first-rate. 'But, what's the matter with Clotilde? On stage she's barely moving. She, who's so lively and so resolute!' Our friend confessed, in fact, that she had been very afraid and that this hampered her exceedingly. The playwright, fearful for the success of his work, tried to persuade Clotilde to shake all the apprehension, to show her real self, and not to think about him at all while she made her delivery. 'I can't help it,' Clotilde responded; 'I'm talking and at the same time I think about you being the playwright and I imagine that the play won't be liked and I get scared.' Inocencio was getting desperate: he pleaded with her, gave her advice, reasoned with her, and caressed her— forgetting that people were watching him; he tried to infuse courage into her by appealing to her pride as an artist; in short, he did everything imaginable to save his play.

"The second act began. Clotilde had some poignant scenes to do. At the outset a little noise arose in the audience, enough to disconcert her and cause her to do them miserably, worse than she had ever done anything in her life. A fair number of coughs and loud murmurs of impatience were heard. As the act ended, some indiscreet friends tried to applaud, but the audience drowned them out with an overpowering and terrifying hissing. The playwright, who was at my side, as white as a sheet, let off steam with a few crude swearwords and retreated to Pepe's room, instead of Clotilde's, where his pals consoled him, blaming her for the fiasco and fanning the flames of bitterness that poured out of his heart. Meanwhile, our poor friend was very affected and depressed, inquiring constantly about her Inocencio. So as not to distress her further, I told her that the playwright had taken it with resignation and had stepped out of the theater to breathe a little fresh air. The poor wretch turned on herself, assuming all the blame.

"The curtain rose for the third act: we all returned to the wings anxiously. Through a mighty effort of the will Clotilde was calmer in the beginning than earlier, but the people were predisposed now to take it all as a joke and nothing could be done to make them serious. An audience, when it has a premonition of turmoil, is the same as a wild beast when it smells blood: there's nobody who can stop it, and meat has to be given to it at all costs. And the truth is that on that occasion it feasted like a glutton. Coughs, bursts of laughter, sneezes, stamps, boos: there was everything. Tears flooded our poor friend's eyes and she was on the verge of fainting. When the curtain descended Clotilde glanced around, looking for her loved one, but he had disappeared. In the dressing room, where I followed her, she wailed, she stamped, she despaired, she called herself stupid; she said she was going to go off to a village to raise chickens, etc., etc. I had an awful time calming her down, but I finally managed it, even though she fell into a deep depression. In the sadness revealed by her eyes I understood that Inocencio's disappearance was tormenting her horribly.

"The door to the room suddenly opened. The poet came in; he was pale, but seemingly unruffled. At first sight I realized, nonetheless, that his calmness was a façade and that the smile contracting his lips bore a resemblance to the one seen on condemned criminals who wish to die with composure.

"A flash of joy lit Clotilde's face. She rose swiftly and threw her arms around his neck, saying to him in a shaken voice:

"'I've ruined you, my poor Inocencio, I've ruined you! How magnanimous you are! But, look, I swear to you, on my father's grave, that I'll make up to you the humiliation you've just suffered.'

"'There's no need for you to make it up to me, darling,' the poet replied quietly, in a tone of voice that betrayed his disdainful anger. 'My family hasn't acquired an illustrious name through the intercession of any actors. From now on I renounce, willingly, the theater and everything associated with it . . . So . . . good-bye.'

"And separating the arms that clung to him and smiling sarcastically, he moved back a few steps and left. Clotilde stared at him in amazement; then she collapsed, unconscious, on the sofa.

"Seeing her in such a state made my blood boil and I went after the young man. I caught up with him near the stairway and grabbed his wrist.

"'Listen, you,' I said to him. 'The first thing that a man should be, before being a poet, is a gentleman . . . and you're not one. The play was booed because it lacks what you lack—a heart. Here's my card.'"

"And did you send him your seconds, Don Jerónimo?" the medical student asked.

"Quiet! Quiet!" exclaimed a member of the group. "Here comes Clotilde."

The winsome actress did in fact appear in the doorway, and her big, sad, black eyes, which stood out beautifully beneath the white Louis XV-style wig, smiled sweetly at her faithful friends.

Merci, Monsieur

It is not good for man to be alone.
—God

When a man lives in a provincial town and has no children and
enjoys a comfortable income and there's a World Fair in Paris,
what choice does he have except to go?

"I assume, Jiménez, that you'll be taking in the fair?"

"Surely you're packing your suitcase?"

"How lucky you are, Don Angel!"

"What will you bring me from the fair, Don Angel?"

I couldn't take it any longer so I caught the train and landed
in Paris. I had no desire whatsoever to visit the fair; industrial
arts have no great attraction for me. I got even less excited about
being stuck on a sixth floor, inside a warm little room with a low
ceiling that looked out on the sky.

Such, however, was the case, and I affirm, with my hand over
my heart, that I would have preferred my own spacious bedroom
which overlooks the garden, my siestas on the old sofa, and my
chocolate made by hand with superior cocoa.

But man is answerable to his fellow citizens, and mine re-
quired this sacrifice and others of me. Every day I came down
from that lofty nest to level ground to go to the fair—eight or ten
kilometers, which I sometimes covered on foot, other times by
omnibus.

One by one I inspected all those pavilions, which did not
awaken the slightest interest in me. One section was filled to the
ceiling with riding boots; another with rolled cable; a third with
carriage lamps; and so on.

I visited them religiously because I realized that it was my
duty. How was I going to return home without being able to state
that I had seen the exhibition of automatic brakes or the display
of Italian soups, etc., etc.?

Tedium began to permeate my spirit. When, at nightfall, I went

91

up to my room and dropped exhausted on the bed, only God knows what black thoughts would cross my mind. Existence, looked at through those colossal exhibitions of mineral fertilizers or firebricks, seemed to me, as it did to Schopenhauer, a monstrous error of the will.

The wind that blew in my attic made my situation even more dreadful. Every night I would hear it sing, threatening to destroy the thin, fragile walls and launch me into outer space.

Finally, on awakening one morning, a fierce instinct of rebellion invaded my entire being. I uttered a terrible oath and exclaimed out loud: "Today I refuse to see cables, brakes, Italian soups, even if . . . !"

Silence! When a man is alone and desperate he sometimes says very ugly things.

I made my toilet and dressed slowly, very slowly, with that concentrated rage of the man who wishes to persuade himself that he's lord and master of his destiny.

I went down to the street and began to stroll along the boulevards like the most inveterate loafer living in Paris at the time. My attitude was that of the person who unexpectedly turns his back on all social obligations, an insolent, aggresive attitude, a look that said to those who crossed my path: 'What do I care?'

Nevertheless, remorse stirred while smothered in my soul, like a bird that's squeezed in one's hand.

I entered a café and asked for an absinthe. In what other drink could I better drown my bitterness?

In contrast, at an adjacent table a pretty French girl with an upturned nose, a narrow forehead, and mischievous eyes, was sipping milk, occasionally dipping small biscuits in it. At her side there were two white-haired men, one of whom must have been her father, judging by the resemblance between them. The old boys chatted animatedly about industrial matters. Mademoiselle was bored to tears.

Now then, when a French girl with an upturned nose gets bored, she's capable of looking with interest at a skeleton, if the skeleton belongs to the masculine sex. Therefore she looked at me, and I, thank God, wasn't one yet.

Suddenly I became all excited, ready to die for her. My heart, shut up for so many days by anguish and impatience, opened like the calyx of a flower to a morning sunbeam. I experienced the oddest sensation, and all my sorrows fled, some through the door, others through the window, like devils chased with holy water.

It was her eyes that sprinkled it, her soft, playful eyes, in which I drank the nectar of love drop by drop. Mine discreetly sang her praises, the thrill of her wavy tresses, the whiteness of her face, the enchantment of her lips, the piquant attractiveness of her little upturned nose. What intelligence animated that divine countenance! She was perfect and she knew it.

But she didn't take advantage of her perfection. Satisfied with her eyes, her hair, and her little nose, she exposed them all to the foreigner's admiration and contrived to make him happy.

She would rest her lips on the rim of the glass, and, raising her eyes at the same time, say to me with them: 'I know, my young foreigner, that it would gratify you to apply your own lips to this very same area to learn my sweet secrets. It's not my fault if you can't do so.' Other times she would straighten her hair slightly. 'I also know that you'd be happy to play with these golden curls, which at this moment are taking away your breath.' Still others, she would extend her dainty hand, as white and delicate as a rosebud, and place it on the back of a chair very close to me. 'You'd like to kiss this small, smooth hand, wouldn't you? Well kiss it, my young foreigner, kiss it with your thoughts since you can't with your lips.'

And I kissed it obediently, I kissed it ardently time and again, until she finally withdrew it, slightly flushed.

'Oh, my lovely little French girl with the mischievious eyes and little upturned nose, I'd like to fly away with you to a far-off land, where carnations bloom under forests of lime trees flooded with sunshine! A white cottage, a meadow that stretches out in front of it, a limpid brook that surrounds it, the ringing of cow-bells, the singing of blackbirds . . . Come, my lovely, come!'

She did, in fact, stand up, but it wasn't due to my conjuration, rather to the two old men, who paid the waiter because they were leaving.

As she crossed in front of me I gallantly withdrew the chair to permit her to pass by unhindered. She glanced at me with a smile on her face and her lips uttered sweetly:

"Merci, monsieur."

'Thank you, Lord!,'[1] I also uttered, raising my thoughts to heaven. 'This French girl is leaving and I'll never see her again, but she has accomplished the mission that You entrusted to her.'

I felt my heart suffused with renewal, imbued with sweet submission. All my obligations seemed easy to fulfill, and, my spirit full of a godliness for which I was grateful, I went out into the street and got on the omnibus to look again at automatic brakes and rolled cable.

---

[1]*Gracias, Señor:* a play on words because *Señor* also means—to parallel *Merci, monsieur*—sir.

Bubbles

A man can behave like a fool in the defiles of a desert, but
every grain of sand seems to see him.
—Emerson

The bully Curro Vázquez, from the region of Jaén, had occasion
quite a few years ago to verify these words of the American philosopher.

Curro Vázquez, even though he had no heart, was in love. This
is a paradox that recurs frequently thanks to the lamentable con-
fusion in which it pleased the Maker to leave physical and moral
concerns.

Pepita Montes, his sweetheart, was completely duped with regard to him. She saw a young, handsome, smiling, humble devoted suitor, and from this she concluded that he was a wingless
angel. She loved him despite her parents, who wished to match
her with a well-off landowner, and not with a horse dealer's sorry
assistant. Because Curro was a pitiable youth whom Francisco
Calderón, the famous horse dealer from Andújar, had taken into
his service some time ago. He plucked him, one can say, out of
the gutter when Curro was only fourteen or fifteen years old,
made him his servant, and eventually his trusted right-hand
man. Calderón paid him handsomely, gave him frequent gifts,
and liked to see him dress stylishly and be well-received by
pretty women.

Curro exploited these advantages and won their love, then deserted them after winning it. But when he met Pepita Montes,
fortune turned the tables and snared *him* in the web of love.
What, however, could he do to marry her given the violent opposition of her brute of a father? This was a question that he had
pondered deeply for three or four months.

After all his soul-searching the only idea that made sense to
him was the vital necessity of making a lot of money, changing

his status as a more or less salaried servant, dealing on his own behalf, etc.

When a man feels the urgent need to get rich quickly, and has no heart, he runs the risk of doing what Curro Vásquez did.

It was a rainy spring afternoon. Francisco Calderón and his servant were returning from the Córdoba fair, wrapped in ponchos as they traversed the sierra on their hacks. Calderón was tickled pink because he had sold five horses at a good price. From time to time he would untie the wineskin filled with amontillado that was fastened to his saddletree, take a long swig, and then give Curro a drink too. Since the rain was getting heavier and they were passing near a hollow in the mountainside, they decided to seek cover for a while and wait for it to stop. They alighted, sheltering their mounts as best they could. Curro unstrapped his double-barreled short rifle and set it next to him.

"What's the rifle for?" his boss asked him, surprised.

"You know that Casares and his band maraud the area."

"Casares! Casares! Casares marauds far away from here, and it's never crossed his mind to come to these parts."

Calderón laughed heartily at his servant's fear.

They sat and calmly smoked. When Curro tossed his cigarette butt, he stood, took the rifle, steadied it against his cheek, and, aiming it at his boss, said to him calmly:

"Mr. Francisco, get ready to die."

Calderón replied that he didn't like jokes with firearms.

"Say the creed, Mr. Francisco."

"What are you talking about?" he exclaimed, trying to get up.

A shot in the chest knocked him on his back.

"You've killed me, you swine!"

"Not yet, but I'm going to," uttered Curro, walking towards him.

"Murderer, you'll be killed too!"

"If there were witnesses, I don't doubt it."

"The bubbles in the water will be witnesses to this . . ."

Another shot sealed his lips forever.

Curro searched through Calderón's pockets, grabbed all the money on him, reloaded his rifle, mounted up, and galloped off.

When he arrived at a suitable site, he again dismounted, and carefully buried the money, marking the spot to enable him to find it. Afterwards he put a bullet through his hat, fired another through the fleshy part of his thigh, and appeared at the first town seemingly in a state of shock. *Casares'* band had surprised them when they were resting and getting ready to resume their journey. Thanks to the fact that he was already mounted he had been able to escape. His boss was still standing there; he didn't know if they had killed him; he had heard numerous shots; he himself had been wounded while fleeing; etc.

The whole story made the judge suspicious, and so, after his recovery in the hospital, Curro was jailed. But since no money was found on him and there were no witnesses, in the end he was set free.

He borrowed some money, so he said, from a horse dealer in Sevilla, and proceeded to work in the same trade as his deceased boss, and he began to prosper. There was some talk, and there were those who suspected the truth, but this kind of thing happens often in small towns and nothing ever comes of it.

And since, in fact, there was no longer any reason to justify his opposition, Pepita Montes' father finally consented to Pepita and Curro's marriage. The wedding was celebrated with pomp and the groom's generosity won him public goodwill.

Business thrived. In a short time Curro became a horse dealer of some importance because he was intelligent and energetic; on the other hand, once he sated his bestial passion, he treated the beautiful Pepita like what he in fact was, a consummate blackguard. Without any reason at all he began to abuse her cruelly in word and deed.

The poor thing suffered the change more surprised than indignant. Since she was hopelessly in love with Curro, the moments of good humor and marital expansiveness compensated her for the bitterness.

But there were fewer and fewer of these moments, and Pepita's life finally became unbearable. During one of them the following took place:

Curro had pulled the wool over an Englishman's eyes and made a terrific sale on a hack. The deal put him in an exceptionally good mood even though the day was one of the dreariest to be seen in Andalucía, overcast and rainy like the weather in the Galician city of Santiago. He had had two bottles of manzanilla brought in, and they had lunched, and made merry, and chattered incessantly. Curro lit a cigarette and went to lean on the window sill; Pepita, feeling tender and affectionate, went over and leaned next to him. With shining eyes and flush faces, both watched the rain fall slowly. Loud trickles that ran down from the rooftop of the house formed little bubbles on the surface of the street.

Curro snorted and let out a snickering chuckle.

"What are you laughing at?" his wife asked him.

"Nothing," he replied with the same smiling countenance.

"At something. You're laughing at me."

And at the same time she affectionately gave him a familiar little pinch.

"Listen, Pepa," he continued, laughing. "Do you think that bubbles in water can be witnesses in a certain situation?"

"What an idea!"

"Well, Mr. Francisco Calderón thought so."

"Mr. Francisco? What does Mr. Francisco have to do with any of this?"

"Yes, before I finished him off with a shot he told me that bubbles would be the witnesses that would denounce me."

"Then you were the one . . . ?"

"You should have guessed it. Do you think that the money in the pocket of one man makes its way to the pocket of another all by itself, as it does in a magician's act?"

And, seized by a sudden and irresistible desire to confess, he recounted the crime in all its detail to his wife.

Pepita was horrified but knew enough to mask her perturbation. Fear on the one hand and the frenetic passion that he still aroused in her on the other, combined to silence the shouts of her conscience. Curro described the execution of his horrible crime with the same calm as if he were relating the incidents of a hunting expedition.

Days passed, and Pepita made tremendous efforts to forget that terrible secret, which to her resembled a nightmare. It was impossible. Curro, for his part, sorry that he had divulged it, watched her suspiciously, gloomily. There seemed to be a vast chasm between them.

The scant affection that he retained for her had vanished with the apprehension. He came to loathe her heartily. Nevertheless, from that point on he refrained from mistreating her.

One night, while they were in bed, he drew the knife that he kept beneath the pillow, held the point to her throat and said:

"If you let slip a single word about *that matter*, you can be certain that I'll slit your throat like a chicken's."

No such thought had entered Pepita's mind.

But in the end abhorrence did its job. One day, because of some insignificant detail concerning lunch, Curro charged his wife and beat her barbarously, and perhaps he would have ended her life (something that deep down he no doubt wished to do), if the miserable creature hadn't managed to elude his grasp, dashing outside and taking refuge in her brother-in-law's house.

The latter, on seeing her in such a state, couldn't help exclaiming:

"That cutthroat wanted to kill you!"

"Yes he wanted to kill me—the same as Mr. Francisco Calderón!"

"What? Curro killed him?"

"Yes, yes, he killed him . . ."

And Pepita told the story word for word, just as Curro had related it to her. Afterwards she tried to retract it, but to no avail. Her brother-in-law, who professed a mortal hatred of Curro, left her locked in a room and went straight to see the judge.

Again Curro was jailed.

The judge, whose suspicions had never disappeared and were now changed into certainty, worked the case with so much zeal and energy, that at length he obliged him to make a full confession.

Some months later Curro ascended the scaffold at Sevilla square. As they fitted the hangman's halter around his neck he was muttering incessantly:

"Bubbles! Bubbles!"

Those who surrounded him thought that terror was making him rave.

Primitive Society

The truth is that to compensate for the games of big people I find nothing more agreeable than the games of little people. The games of the former are tiresome, harmful and melancholy, in particular, politics; those of the latter are cheerful, expressive, and full of profound lessons. Therefore, when I take a walk in Retiro Park I'm accustomed to sitting on one of the wood benches (never on the stone ones, for reasons that I prefer not to disclose) where I pass the time very pleasantly observing the bustle of children.

In this small world, as in the other one, all kinds of passions exist, from base envy to sublime heroism; on display are love, jealousy, arrogance, courage, and fear. But all of them are delightful and enchanting because all of them are natural. Nature does not produce ugly qualities—it is our despicable thinking that introduces them in life.

Also, the scenes that I witness transport me to the world in its infancy and to the beginnings of human society. What unrestrained freedom to initiate and terminate relationships! Cordial friendship, open hatred, acknowledged envy, ostensible vanity, and avowed fear. It is a primitive society; it is the human being who is independent and free, who controls his existence and revels in it.

A little girl crossed in front of me walking slowly, almost solemnly, as she glanced complacently in all directions. She was an adorable little creature about six or seven years old, blond like an ear of corn. Her mama was undoubtedly fond of flowers. She looked at them and then looked again, stopping in front of each one, occasionally stroking them with a little hand so white and so exquisite that it did not pale alongside them. Her mama was accomplished in gardening? Well, she was too, and she demonstrated her competence by trimming with little scissors the flowers' excess leaves.

And she was more than a little proud of the scissors that hung from a blue silk ribbon tied to her waist. With what pleasure she watched them swing in step with her stride! What joy could be seen in her blue eyes as she used them to cut away carefully the excess leaves!

But were those leaves really excess? This is what a caretaker with a huge, black mustache wondered. He shouted at her in a formidable voice:

"Hey, little girl! Be careful with touching the flowers because I'll take you to the Office and lock you up in jail."

The child turned pale and rigid. Virgin of Atocha!* The Office! Jail! And never again see her mama or Melita or Chichí! Fortunately Pepa, her longtime day nurse, came on the run and shook her by the arm.

"Angelina! What have you done? You foolish, foolish little thing. What nerve! Don't you know that the flowers aren't to be touched?"

Undoubtedly neither that ugly caretaker nor Pepa had any knowledge of gardening because her mama frequently cut the leaves of the flowers on the terrace.

The caretaker left displeased, Pepa left displeased, and Angelina was also displeased. But it didn't take long for her to recover her gaiety. She quickly forgot about her crime, deploring, and rightly so, the lack of horticultural expertise on the part of certain people, and continued to inspect the city's most recent plantings, but leaving her little scissors at her side.

A little further away there was a group of boys, none of whom could have been more than ten, who were enthusiastically engaged in inflating a fairly small hot air balloon. They had hung it from the branch of a tree and were setting fire to pieces of paper which they placed inside of it until they were completely burned, and then they would start all over again and repeat the process. What a frivolous activity! What childishness! Angelina, with her superior sense of esthetics, glanced pityingly at them from time to time.

Among the balloon inflators, the one who worked most energetically and seemed to be directing the operation was a boy of robust complexion wearing a sailor suit. He had big, black, fierce eyes, and his hair was also black and fell in curls over his sweating forehead. From his imperious gestures, fearful glances, and grave bearing, it was clear that he was an oriental despot in miniature. The others obeyed him without argument.

Angelina, still inspecting her flowers, happened to pass near them. One of the boys looked at her out of the corner of his eye, smiled, and mumbled a few words in the ear of the one closest to him, who in turn also smiled and said a few words in the ear of the one on the other side of him. They all interrupted their work and contemplated the little garden fairy with smiles on their faces. That is to say, not all of them: the chief of the tribe stared haughtily at her and immediately turned away to resume his task.

Angelina felt the full force of those mocking smiles and she blushed.

But . . . what were they saying to each other? What were those mischievous boys scheming? Angelina didn't know but she observed that they were talking to each other without taking their eyes off her, and she guessed that a plot was being hatched against her person. She gazed about anxiously and noticed with terror that Pepa was at quite a distance and engaged in conversation with other servants. Those primitive little beings, in whom the dawn of ethical behavior was just beginning to appear, were capable of anything.

And sure enough, without giving her time to flee, the boys suddenly surrounded her; they hemmed her in, let out savage screams, laughed brutally, like the heroes of the *Odyssey*, and finally their audacity reached the extreme of putting their lips on the adorable little girl's face.

Indignation outweighed fear, which has always been the case with all Christian maidens.

"I'll jab you! I'll jab you!" she began to shout, brandishing her little scissors.

But she did not actually do it because she had developed a larger sense of humanity and was horrified at the thought of spilling the blood of a fellow human being.

The barbarians cleverly took advantage of that delicate moral sense and one after another kissed, while laughing, those innocent cheeks.

But behold: heavenly justice, disguised in the bodily and mortal figure of Pepa, fell unexpectedly on them. A slap in the face here, a blow on the neck there, a tug on one's ear, a pull on another's hair, all of this in much less time than it takes to describe, and the riffraff was dispersed. By virtue of momentum (we prefer to give her the benefit of the doubt), Pepa also lit into

Anglina and delivered two slaps on those rosy cheeks that were kissed repeatedly only moments before.

The savages cried, their victim cried, and—admirable example—celestial justice also cried. From fury? From remorse?

A minute later, however, it was as if nothing had happened. The savages, halfway satisfied with their escapade, returned to their task of inflating the balloon, and Angelina was dragged to the servants' court to be judged. Not even a hint of guilty conduct turned up. She was, therefore, freely absolved with favorable pronouncements all around.

With her eyes cleaned and her cheeks rubbed to a bright red to erase any trace of those gross kisses, Angelina, like a carefree and pert little bird, inspected the flowers again. Little by little she approached once again the Bohemians' camp and passed repeatedly in front of them. "Oh feminine flirtation that bursts forth so soon in the heart of a seven year old!" you readers will exclaim philosophically. Naturally, that's what I thought, but I soon became convinced that I was doing the charming creature a disservice. What drove her again toward the tribe's territory was not coquetry, but a vivid sense of justice.

In spite of the astonishment and distress that the barbarians' aggression caused her, Angelina managed to observe that their leader, the striking boy with black eyes and black hair, had not taken part in the commotion. He had not moved from his spot, observing with a derisive and disdainful expression his companions' villainy.

Angelina, passing in front of the group, shot penetrating glances at him that were full of curiosity and gratitude. I saw her hesitate, take a step toward him and then retrace it; finally, she approached in a resolute manner and said to him:

"You were good, and because you were, I'm going to give you a kiss."

And true to her word, she put her coral lips on the chief's tan cheek. Immobile like a statue, he allowed himself to be kissed, cast a long and proud glance at her and, turning up his nose, returned to his task with the same eagerness as before.

A Witness for the Prosecution

There are people who take a walk only in the center of the city. There are others who prefer the outlying, solitary streets where Madrid's periphery borders on open country. And there are those, lastly, who shun both areas and only find happiness measuring the halls of their homes with long strides, approaching the stove every now and then to warm their hands.

Well, I declare that I belong to the second group, although I too enjoy pacing the hall with my hands in my pockets, especially when it rains, and I like taking a few turns along Alcalá and Sevilla streets during the rush hours. When the latter is the case, I try to keep a frown and a stormy look on my face in order to adapt to the environment, but it goes against my grain, as God well knows, because my facial expression is by nature serene and tender.

I experience, therefore, more pleasure taking a walk on the outskirts, where I encounter happy faces that look at me without hostility. Only there do I relax and am I outwardly what God tried to make of me. And I've thought several times that if we transferred the faces of the outskirts to the center, and sent packing those of the latter, Madrid would present to the eyes of foreigners a more hospitable, more cheerful, and, above all, a more humane appearance than the one it now has.

With dogs it's a different story. Generally I find those of the center gentle and well-behaved; those of the outlying areas aggressive, bad-tempered, and much more unkempt in their personal cleanliness. Undoubtedly, culture, which exercises such a sorry influence on the human race, mellows and enhances the canine.

I don't know if the dog that I ran into one day in one of the most out-of-the way streets of the Chamberí district was troublesome and aggressive like his fellows, but I can testify to his shocking filthiness. Skinny and woolly, like those Bohemians who never trim their beards and let them grow like weeds, cov-

104

ered with dust and matted with mud, this repugnant animal approached me wagging his tail and looking at me meekly.

I jumped backwards because experience has taught me that they can wag their tails humbly and still be at bottom dangerous creatures. I soon became convinced that there was nothing to fear. That poor dog had fallen on such hard times, was so helpless and beaten, that the last embers of his sour temper, if he had ever had one, had been completely extinguished.

I snapped my fingers softly, in unison with his dizzying tail-wagging, and got ready to continue on my way; but he thanked me for that indifferent attention as nobody had ever in my life thanked me for the most affectionate, cordial greeting. He began to jump up and down in front of me and wiggle, and emit soft, insinuating howls, expressing as much joy as gratitude.

In this base world thanks are not offered in such a manner—I was again reminded by experience—unless something is feared or hoped for. This dog has no master, or has been thrown out of the house by him! Poor thing! His misfortune awakened my curiosity, and again I snapped my fingers, somewhat more effusively this time, and it caused him to renew his display of appreciation almost to the point of dislocating himself.

He immediately decided to follow me to the end of the world.

Several times I saw him behind, escorting me; other times he went ahead, acting as my herald. Occasionally he would stop, raising his hairy snout towards me and looking at me with affectionate submission, as if he wanted to say that he was prepared to obey me as lord and master. His misfortune moved me. He was so ugly that there was no reason to be surprised that his owner had abandoned him.

And, nevertheless, I've seen some wealthy women caress and pamper other dogs uglier than this one with passionate transports of love, and I've also seen some elegant young men caress and pamper these same women, uglier still than their dogs.

I pictured that poor animal, ignominiously thrown out of his home, returning to it to seek pity, howling mournfully at the door; I saw him, lost and hungry, wandering along those lonely streets, entering a shop in search of scraps and coming out beaten up, following passersby until they chased him off with kicks or stones.

My heart went out to that dog, and when he stopped to look

at me, I would make gestures of friendship to him. Then he'd come up to me, overflowing with gratitude, and unafraid of soiling my hands, I patted his head like the charitable saints of legend.

But as time went by, a vague disquiet was taking hold of me. What was I going to do with that poor devil? You don't give alms to a dog nor recommend him to a town councilor friend for a job as a city laborer. I needed to take him home with me. That was serious. What would the doorman say, what would the neighbors say, what, most of all, would my family say on seeing that ugly, disgusting animal come in? What protests, what commotion, what ridicule would be stirred up at home! I got goose bumps.

Immediately I comprehended the absurdity of my situation.

I then did to that dog what my friends do to me when my presence disturbs them: I pretended not to notice him. When he looked at me with his affectionate eyes, I would frown as if I didn't see him and continue on my way. Finally, I assumed an air as icy as it was expressive, but he didn't see its significance or refused to see it. Not taking the hint, he persisted in his indications of unconditional attachment, always considering himself under my protection.

One of the times that our glances crossed, I saw in the dog's eyes an expression of such surprise and supplication that my heart sank. Nevertheless, what he was asking wasn't possible.

My uneasiness continued to increase and I entertained the barbaric step of violently flinging him from my side, when I noticed that a streetcar was coming towards us. Then, stealthily, I grabbed hold of it and climbed on. From the platform I saw my dog, who was walking calmly and trustingly, suddenly turn around: he was surprised and sniffed the air in desperation. Finally, he lowered his head again towards the ground, resigned, like those beings who have experienced all the grief in this world and know what can be expected from existence.

I never could forget that animal, and on remembering him I can't help thinking that some day, when I stand before the high court of God, and all the acts of my life are judged and all my shortcomings and mistakes are tallied, I'll see him appear with his hairy snout and aggrieved look to bear witness to my cruel selfishness.

Perico the Good

Our ideals do not always conform to the secret tendencies of our nature, as moralistic philosophers claim. On the contrary, in many cases I've seen a tremendous disparity surface.

I've known misers who profoundly admired spendthrifts, who would have given everything in the world to be like them . . . except money. There was a merchant in my town who spent his entire life relating to us what he had squandered on a trip that he had made to Paris, on his sprees, and the prodigious number of *louis** that he had lavished on mundane beauties. The good man shed tears of joy narrating his imaginary adventures. But this is a story that I'll leave for another time.

Now I'm going to tell you Perico's, known as Perico the Good. None of us in the town knew where this nickname came from, and he least of all, for it aroused unspeakable anger in him. There wasn't a more unruly, mischievous boy in the school. He was the teachers' nightmare and the porters' and beadles' terror. As soon as a riot or disturbance arose in the yard, you could take for granted that Perico would be in the middle of it; if there were slaps, Perico was the one who gave them; if yells and curses were heard, nobody other than he shouted them.

I can picture him with a black cigar in his mouth, strolling along the porticos with his hands in his pockets and casting insolent glances at the beadles.

"Mr. Baranda," one of them would say to him courteously, "be kind enough to remove that cigar from your mouth: the principal will be coming this way momentarily."

"Tell the principal to kiss me right here," Perico would respond fiercely.

The beadle would pounce on Perico and seize him by the neck to throw him in the coal cellar which doubled as a cell. Perico would resist and then the janitor would lend a hand; between the two men, and after an arduous effort, they managed to drag Perico off and leave him locked up there.

I can also picture him in Psychology, Logic and Ethics class, shooting paper arrows and making us laugh with his funny faces. The teacher was a plump, kind little man, fond of similes.

"Mr. Baranda, just as the rotten apple is separated from the others in order not to spoil the bushel, kindly move away from your classmates and sit in that corner on the right."

Perico wouldn't budge an inch from his place.

"Mr. Baranda, please move," the teacher would repeat.

"Let the good apples move," Perico would retort, shrugging his shoulders in a disdainful manner.

The teacher would insist, trying to persuade him with reasons and threats. It all came to naught. Finally, he would say to us, a little ashamed:

"Well, well. Kindly move away and leave him alone."

And there we were, the thirty or forty of us boys who constituted the class getting up out of our seats and moving five or six feet away from the rebel.

Of course I'm sure that he wasn't disciplined and expelled from the school forever out of respect for his father, Don Pedro Baranda. This gentleman was a manufacturer who owned a brick factory on the outskirts of the town, an excellent person and, moreover, one of the leaders of the Republican party. Since we were in the middle of a revolution no teacher dared to incur his displeasure.

Perico suffered horribly every time he heard himself called the *Good*. He would gnash his teeth, and if it was some boy his age who insulted him in this manner, he would lunge at him and sock him on the nose. Because it should be pointed out that Perico was pugnacious and, although not very strong, marvelously agile and dexterous in all kinds of exercises. Nobody surpassed him in running and jumping and nobody excelled in leapfrog and other games like him. I remember that one afternoon a number of us played hooky at his instigation, and instead of going to our Rhetoric and Poetics class we went out in the country to wander around. Because we had gone too far and dusk had come upon us, we were afraid that we wouldn't be back by the Angelus bell, which were our parents' standing instructions. We were near the bridge that the railroad tracks crossed. Perico saw a train coming at full speed and, without saying a word to us, climbed the guardrail and jumped on one of the car platforms, thereby managing to reach the town safe and sound in a matter of minutes.

Why shouldn't I acknowledge it? I admired him and I was his true friend. He always showed a special predilection for me too, and in my company gave vent to his sorrows. One of the greatest was that ridiculous nickname that weighed upon him. He thought it the height of humiliation.

"Imagine," he'd say to me now and then, smiling bitterly, "calling me Perico the Good when I'm the *baddest* person around."

He couldn't remove this thorn from his side.

After we graduated I lost track of Perico. I came to Madrid and he stayed in our home town. Some years later I found him a thoroughly changed person. His father had died, he had taken charge of the factory, and he had entered politics. He was a serious, silent man, but always energetic and ready to get angry over the slightest thing. He held extremely radical, almost anarchistic, political ideas, and when the time came he expressed them with a vehemence and cynicism that astonished and alarmed the peaceful inhabitants of our town. Discussion of religion was better avoided: he had declared himself an avowed enemy of the Maker, and at the conclusion of a binge with his sidekicks he would talk—as if it were a natural, simple act—of drinking the blood of the last king from the skull of the last priest.

And, nevertheless, in the town he continued to be called Perico the Good! Of course it was behind his back, because nobody would have dared to voice this offensive nickname to his face.

He delivered speeches at the workingmen's club and harangued the masses at the Republican demonstrations with much more ardor than eloquence. His spirit found nourishment only in the editorials of radical newspapers and the books of the latest materialistic philosophers. Büchner's *Force and Matter** was his bible. But just recently, not long before my return home, some of the works of Friedrich Nietzsche had fallen into his hands, works which he had devoured like a true glutton; without digesting them very well, he made use of the ideas to terrify his neighbors. For him all virtues were the object of fierce, sarcastic remarks: kindness only meant weakness; humility, baseness; and patience, cowardice. On the other hand, he extolled cruelty, cunning, rash audacity, and an aggressive character as precious instincts that increase our vitality and make life more beautiful and intense.

"It's necessary to say *Yes* to evil and sin!" he would repeat constantly at the Casino, in the midst of the stupefaction of the innocent middle-class citizens who listened to him. He spoke of demolishing hospitals, asylums, and poor houses as centers of putrefaction where we carefully preserve human decay that afterwards is spread and poisons all of us; he expressed his enthusiasm for the Spartan custom of hurling deformed children over a precipice, and even found reasonable another one which consigned the aged and infirm to sacrifice . . . In short, a real horror.

If one of those present tried to cut him off and respond to such atrocities, Perico would get incensed and rant so much and so loudly that you had to leave him alone.

One afternoon, at the Casino, he was taking pleasure in attacking and ridiculing saintliness, repeating the paradoxes of the philosopher who had turned his head.

"There exist certain men," he was saying, "who feel such an intense need to exercise their power and their tendency towards domination that, for want of other objects, or because they've always been a failure, end up by tyrannizing some part of their own being. Saintliness, in the final analysis, is a question of vanity."

Unfortunately, it occurred to an erudite teacher from the secondary school to rebut him.

"But Mr. Baranda, is there any man on this earth so bereft of power that he cannot make his fellow creatures feel it in some way? I've known maimed beggars and sick persons, people plunged into the most profound abasement, who would leave lighted matches in haylofts and put pieces of glass on roads so that pedestrians would hurt themselves."

Perico repressed his anger with difficulty and tried to speak calmly.

"I'm telling you that it's a question of vanity and, furthermore, passion. Under the influence of a violent emotion man can decide on a course of frightful revenge the same as a course of frightful annihilation of his need for revenge. In one or the other case, it's only a matter of relieving excitement."

"But passion is no more than exaltation of feeling," the teacher declared. "For there to exist a religious excitement capable of producing asceticism it is first necessary for religious feeling to have existed. It isn't, then, religious passion that you should explain to us, rather the feeling from which it stems. That man, overcome and dominated by excessive excitement, can decide to behave in a monstrous and even nocuous manner, is a foregone conclusion. But *why* and *how* such excitement has been produced is what we ought to look into. If in some cases the effects of love and hate can be the same, since the fire of exaltation consumes and obliterates the differences, not on that account will they cease to be radically different and opposite feelings."

"All right; but even if it weren't a question of vanity and passion, I can't help profoundly despising those castrates," Perico replied in a contemptuous tone and gesture. "After all, those eunuchs, incapable of enjoying life, only try to make it more bearable by submitting abjectly to another's will or to a rule. They are, at bottom, Epicureans, although quite ludicrous ones."

"A strange way to make life agreeable—obeying a capricious, irascible or stupid superior!" the teacher exclaimed. "And even if they willed themselves not to feel the resentment caused by humiliation, how would they avoid the suffering that results from physical discomforts? Is life more tolerable for the person who doesn't have a moment to himself, who's forced to eat dishes that revolt him, to sit up at night when he's sleepy, to sleep when he isn't, to travel when he's tired and rest when he feels a need to be active, than for one who enjoys freedom of movement? The philosopher Epicurus would be astonished, surely, to have St. Anthony and St. Francis considered his disciples. Because if for him intellectual and moral serenity denoted the greatest pleasure in life, he likewise judged physical well-being as a condition for moral tranquility, and the pleasures of the body, especially those of the palate, as the root of the pleasures of the spirit."

The Casino members took the teacher's part and this so inflamed Perico that he began to argue in a loud voice and use coarse expressions, as was his practice since childhood. To such a degree that his interlocutor, his patience finally exhausted, shrugged his shoulders disdainfully and refused to continue the discussion.

Not many weeks afterwards, while quite a few people were walking along the sidewalk on Constitution Square, a raging fire broke out in the Traditionalist Club, which was housed in a two-story building on the very same square. It was dusk at the time and the few members who were there quickly rushed outside. The janitor had left on an errand. A throng crowded in front of it and then began the extinguishing work, which amounted to no more than some men climbing on adjacent roofs with pitchers of water to prevent the fire from spreading to other houses. They were waiting for the firemen, who were a long time in coming.

The fire was terrible, with flames leaping out the windows, when all of a sudden heart-rending wails rose in the street. A woman, disheveled and as pallid as a corpse, was running toward the house, screaming:

"My children! My children!"

It was the janitor's wife, whose family lived on the upper floor. Nobody had realized that there were four children shut up inside, the oldest of whom was seven. She tried to rush the door, but several people restrained her; flames were licking at the staircase and she was headed for a certain death.

"Where are your children?" asked Baranda, who had a tight grip on her arm.

"There! There!" the anguished woman shouted, pointing to the right of the building. "Let go of me, for God's sake!"

Perico Baranda let go of her, but it was to rush towards the barred windows of the ground floor and scale the balconies of the second with the agility of a monkey. The crowd watched him disappear and then reappear a minute later with a little girl in his arms. Everybody let out a shout of joy. A ladder was positioned nearby and the child taken from him.

Perico intrepidly dashed back inside. Shortly afterwards he emerged with another little girl, his clothing scorched and his face blackened.

"Wet me down, for God's sake! Wet me down, wet me down!" he shouted in a hoarse voice.

Several buckets of water were thrown at him from adjacent roofs, but none reached him. A man climbed the ladder with a pail and poured water over his head.

Perico rushed back inside again in spite of the fact that flames enveloped him and the collapse of the roof was imminent.

Shortly afterwards he appeared with another child.

This time he emerged so disfigured that he could barely be recognized. Immediately apparent was that he had injured his hands and face, and it looked as if he were going to fall faint.

"Wet me down, wet me down!"

"Enough already, Perico, enough!" several people shouted.

"It's not enough, damn you, because there's still another child inside!" Perico roared.

And as soon as they had thrown another pail of water over his head, he dashed back into the inferno.

A terrible moment of anguish! Every heart was beating frantically. One second more . . .

A horrible noise was heard. The roof had crashed down, and Perico did not come out again. The people cried out in grief, and tears were streaming down everybody's cheeks.

The following day they found his charred body embracing that of a child a few months old.

Those precious remains were laid to rest in a gilded coffin. The entire town, young and old, women and children, followed it to the cemetery. Transport of the coffin, covered with wreaths, was constantly interrupted because men contended with one another for the honor of carrying it on their shoulders, even if it was only for a minute.

When the coffin reached its destination it was buried, literally, amid flowers.

The instinct of the townspeople hadn't been mistaken. The mayor, interpreting it, had these simple words inscribed on his tomb:

HERE LIES PERICO THE GOOD.

The Life of a Canon

My uncle Don Sebastián had much more decided ideas about the asceticism of canons than did Pachón from Quintana de Arriba. No hesitations on this point: he knew where he stood. For him, the person of a canon evoked countless bountiful, delightful, and cozy images.

It's not surprising. If there was talk of a really invigorative mellow wine, he heard it called "canon's wine"; if the topic was an exquisite chocolate, "canon's chocolate"; if it was a soft, stuffed mattress, a "canon's mattress"; etc.

All his life he had felt a base envy for the upper echelon of the clergy, and bitterly regretted that his father had not devoted him to ecclesiastic life, instead of leaving him in charge of the hardware business that they operated on the ground floor of the house. Because if he had sent him to the seminary, maybe Don Sebastián would be a canon now. Why not? Hadn't his cousin Gaspar become one, Gaspar who was considered a dimwit in school? And no less than archdeacon of León's holy cathedral church!

It was true that the treatment given him by his sisters wasn't designed to rid his flesh of concupiscent appetites. Those two sisters that his father had left him along with the hardware business were ferocious. It's not known if they had planned to get rich at the expense of the above-mentioned flesh of their brother or if they thought with terror about his death and the necessity of selling the business, or, who knows, perhaps about his marriage. Because even though my uncle Don Sebastián had never exhibited matrimonial whims, when least expected any good-for-nothing could entrap him. The woman who marries a man with two spinster sisters is always a good-for-nothing. In any event, these two sisters scrimped on his bread, meat, and wine, on his shoe blacking, towels for drying and even water for washing.

And in this manner the three had lived beyond the age of forty. Don Sebastián, whom nature had endowed with an easygoing, voluptuous temperament, indulged himself in some treats when he could, behind the backs of those two awful viragos. One day he would go off with Don Hermenegildo, the first mate, to the Moral to eat a basket of barnacles and drink a few liters of cider; another day he would cleverly slip into Cazana's shop and have a filled doughnut and a half bottle of Rueda wine, or else in the afternoon he'd go to the Imperial Café and ask for a strawberry sherbet.

But the two disagreeable virgins had news of all these transgressions the following day. Their police force was more efficient and more faithful than that of the sultan of Turkey. Good heavens, what a scandal, what a scene, what frightful imprecations! On a certain occasion one of the sisters even gave him a formidable whack on the head with a broom.

My uncle Don Sebastián found a way to avenge fully, and in one stroke, all these outrages. Just ask any old man from the town and he'll relate the story to you, half out of breath with laughter. It happened as follows:

One day Don Sebastián went upstairs from the shop with a letter in his hand. It was from cousin Gaspar. He wrote that he was in Oviedo spending some time with the bishop, who, before being preconized had been his companion and close friend in León; at the same time he informed them that he would come on the next day's diligence to pay a visit and spend a few days with them.

The disturbance that this news produced in the two spinsters was indescribable. To have as a guest the archdeacon of León, a close friend of the bishop, at whose table he sat and with whom he secretly used the familiar form of address, according to rumors! They no longer remembered the cousin Gaspar whose trousers they mended so that his mother wouldn't tan his hide if he came home with them torn, and to whom they had given a fair number of smacks on the neck, calling him an idiot. For the two women there only existed now a distinguished celebrity who overflowed with theology and respectability.

After the first impression of astonishment had passed, both spinsters were galvanized into an awesome amount of domestic activity. They removed their corsets, tied scarves around their heads, and themselves began the cleaning and arrangement of the "guest room." The great lignum vitae bed with its canopy and bedspread of red damask was the object of a meticulous inspection. They thoroughly beat the fan palm mattress and feather pillows, put on embroidered sheets of fine cambric, that had never in living memory left the linen closet, and spread along one side a lovely carpet that another, deceased, cousin had brought them from Manila.

The maid was sent off in different directions. To Nepomuceno's confectionery to order a cake, half almond, half borage; to the market of Facunda, the fishwife, to have her select several dozen oysters and deliver them promptly at eleven the next morning; to the glass factory to ask Don Napoleón, the foreman, to leave at daybreak to hunt a few woodcocks, etc., etc.

My uncle Don Sebastián followed these preparations with respectful attention, not daring to utter a single word. The slightest remark would suffice for him to be called a goose, and he had no desire to serve as a pretext for this zoological comparison.

The following day he got suitably dressed up in the morning and left at eleven-thirty to wait for the diligence from Oviedo, which always arrived at noon. The table was already set: a dazzling table, with an old and valuable service crammed with candies and fruit preserves. Don Sebastián returned with bowed head at a quarter after twelve, saying that cousin Gaspar had not arrived on the diligence from Oviedo. The most profound dejection showed on the two sisters' faces. A few moments of painful silence went by. Finally, Don Sebastián exclaimed in a funereal tone:

"I think he must have missed the morning diligence. Surely he'll arrive on the afternoon one . . ."

These simple and reasonable words were enough for his two sisters to confront him like two wild beasts and call him . . . Why say what they called him?

In any case, there was no alternative except to sit down at the table and eat. Don Sebastián did so in grand style. His sisters talked away like the two chatterboxes that they were, making the most absurd comments about the situation. He gulped his food in silence, deliberately and expertly, bringing joy to the delectable mouthfuls with sips of wine from Las Navas. After dessert Don Sebastián rose from his chair as if he had carried out a painful duty, and left, as always, for the Casino. When he turned the corner of the street he lit one of the cigars that he had purchased for the archdeacon, and, puffing it sensually, went off to play his game of omber.

The canon did not arrive on the seven o'clock diligence either. Don Sebastián conveyed the unfortunate news to his sisters with the same countenance that he would have read the death sentence to them. Consternation paralyzed everybody's tongue. There were no comments, no protests, no laments. A somber silence descended on the distressed family.

But the table was set. Salmon, stewed woodcocks, kidneys in sherry sauce, chicken breast béchamel, quince compote, spiked sponge cake, strawberries and cream. Don Sebastián cast furtive, anxious glances at such a rich feast. His sisters, captives of a silent desperation, showed no signs of going near it.

"Well, let's have dinner . . . In any case, the food's paid for . . ."

These words provoked a lachrymal crisis, after which the three sat down at the table. The sisters ate against their will, exhaling pitiful sighs; the brother ate eagerly, imbibing exquisite drinks.

When they rose, Don Sebastián was tottering. Pain usually produces these depressing effects. To disperse it a little, he said he was going to take a stroll along the pier. When he turned the corner he lit again another of the magnificent Havana cigars intended for the archdeacon, and went to sit down on one of the park benches, where he stayed until the chilly air chased him home.

His sisters had already shut themselves in their bedroom. The house was quiet and gloomy, as if misfortune weighed upon it.

My uncle Don Sebastián undressed slowly; but instead of getting in his bed, he took the candlestick in his hand, leaned out in the hall with it and, after ensuring that nobody was watching him, covered very stealthily the distance that separated him from the "guest room" and slid inside the great lignum vitae bed.

Oh, sweet, soft mattress! Oh, downy pillows! Oh, exquisite sheets!

My uncle Don Sebastián felt a heavenly happiness wash over him. He blew out the light, closed his eyes, and murmured, smiling at the darkness:

"Now I won't die without having experienced the life of a canon."

I Puritani*

He was an elegant, refined gentleman with pleasant features and an open manner. I had no reason to refuse to share my room with him for a few days. The landlord of the boardinghouse introduced him to me as a former lodger to whom he was much indebted. He told me that if I refused to take the man in he would be forced to turn him away because there wasn't an empty room in the house, and he would regret this very much indeed.

"Well, if he isn't going to be in Madrid any more than a few days, and if he doesn't go to bed and get up at odd hours, I have no objection to your installing a bed in the anteroom . . . But mind you, this is highly unusual!"

"Don't worry, sir, I won't inconvenience you again with a similar request. I'm doing it only to keep Don Ramón from having to go elsewhere. Believe me—he's a good person, a saint, and won't trouble you at all."

And it was the truth. In the fifteen days that Don Ramón spent in Madrid I had no reason to regret my willingness to help. He was an exemplary roommate. If he returned home later than I, he would come in and go to bed so quietly that not once did he wake me. If he turned in first, he would read and wait up for me so that I could go to bed without fear of making noise. In the morning he never got up until he heard me cough or move around in bed. He lived near Valencia, in a country house, and only came to Madrid when he had to; this time it was to negotiate the promotion of a son, a recorder of deeds. In spite of the fact that this son was my age, Don Ramón wasn't a day over fifty, which led me to believe that he had married rather young, as was indeed the case.

He must have been quite handsome at the time. Even now— tall, with a curly, neatly trimmed gray beard, bright sparkling eyes, and wrinkle-free skin—many women would prefer him to suitors still wet behind the ears.

Don Ramón had, like me, the odd habit of singing or humming

while washing. But I noticed after just a few days that, although he chose and discarded at random various operatic and musical comedy passages, destroying and demolishing them between highs and lows, the piece that he tackled with the most ardor and most often, was from *I Puritani*. I think it was the baritone's aria in the first act. Don Ramón didn't know the lyrics all that well, but he sang the piece with the same gusto that he would have if he had known them. He always began with:

> Il sogno beato
> di pace e contento
> ti, ro, ri, ra, ri, ro,
> ti, ro, ri, ra, ri, ro

He would need to continue humming until coming to two other lines:

> La dolce memoria
> di un tenero amore.*

These he would repeat nonstop until the conclusion of the *allegro*.

"So, Don Ramón," I said to him one day from my bed, "it seems that you like *I Puritani*."

"Very much. It's one of the operas that I like the most. I'd give anything to know an instrument well enough to play the entire work. What a sweet sound it has! What inspiration! This is real opera and this is real music. It seems impossible that you and others get excited about that German gibberish that's only good for putting people to sleep! I'm passionately fond of all of Bellini's operas—*Il pirata, La sonnambula, Norma*, but most especially of *I Puritani*. Besides, I have personal reasons for preferring it to any other," he added, lowering his voice.

"You don't say!" I exclaimed, bounding up in bed and putting on my socks. "Let's hear those reasons, Don Ramón."

"The tomfoolery of youth . . . , amorous escapades," he responded, blushing a little.

"Well, tell me about this foolish behavior. I love these things. I can't help it—I'd rather listen to something like this than the reform of the mortgage law, which you discussed yesterday."

"In the end a poet!"

"I'm not a poet, Don Ramón, I'm a critic."

"Well, the landlord informed me that you were a poet. At any rate, since you're curious, I'll tell the story. You'll see that it's a piece of foolishness, and not worth the trouble. But, get dressed, young man—you're freezing!

"In 1858 I came to Madrid on assignment from the municipal government of Valencia to negotiate a reduction of the food tax. At the time I was . . . , let's see, twenty-nine years old, and I had been married for exactly seven. It's barbaric to marry so young. Although I have no cause for regret, I wouldn't advise anybody to do it.

"I ended up at this same boardinghouse, that is, at this same establishment; at that time the actual business was in a building located on Barquillo Street. I should point out to you that in those days I used to enjoy going around like a veritable jackanapes or dandy, as you say now, which always made my wife wary. 'Good heavens, man, why do you dress up to kill? To make conquests?' 'Who knows!' I would answer, laughing, and angering her a little. It doesn't hurt for women to be a bit jealous.

"One afternoon, one of those lovely winter afternoons that you only see here in Madrid, I went out with the aim of paying a few visits and also to delight in being in the city. I was strolling slowly along Infantas Street, thinking about what I'd do that evening, that is, the best way to enjoy myself, and relishing a good Havana cigar, when suddenly—crash—I receive a nasty bang on the head that makes me reel. My magnificent top hat went rolling in one direction and my cigar in another. When I recovered from the scare the first thing that I saw at my feet was an enormous pink doll, new and dressed in a nightgown.

"This is the villain, this is the one who's caused the damage, I said to myself, shooting an angry glance at it, which the doll pretended not to understand. But since I had to presume that it had not, of its own volition, hurled itself at me in such a brusque, unceremonious manner—because I had never harmed any doll anywhere—I thought it more likely that someone had thrown it at me from a house. I abruptly raised my head.

"Sure enough, the culprit was standing on a second-floor balcony looking bewildered, flabbergasted, astounded. It was a thirteen or fourteen-year-old girl.

"On observing her frightened, anguished expression, my fury

subsided and, instead of rebuking her severely, which was my intention, I presented her with a gallant smile. It's quite possible that the criminal's uncommon beauty contributed more or less directly to the formation of that smile.

"I retrieved my hat, put it on, raised my head again, and gave her another smile, accompanied this time by a slight bow. But my assailant was still motionless and terrified, without noticing or being able to fathom her victim's amiable disposition. While this was going on, the doll lay on the ground, also motionless, but without showing any surprise, regret, fright or embarrassment at its not very decorous situation. I hastened to pick it up, grasping it, if my memory serves me right, by a leg, and I examined it meticulously to determine if it had sustained a fracture or some other serious injury. But it only showed slight bruises. I then held the doll high and showed it to its owner, signaling to her that I was going to go up and return it to her. So without further delay, I entered the hall, climbed the stairs, and pulled the bell cord. My pretty assailant with the olive complexion and the charming, animated, youthful face appeared at the already open door; she extended her tiny hands, into which I respectfully deposited the unconscious doll. I wanted to talk, to assure her even further, that what had happened was nothing, that the doll's members were intact, as were mine, and that I welcomed the opportunity to meet such a nice, beautiful girl, etc., etc. None of this was possible. She mumbled something like "Thank you very much" and hurriedly closed the door, leaving me with my speech undelivered.

"I went out into the street a little vexed, like any other orator in a similar situation, and continued on my way, not without repeatedly looking back at the balcony. Thirty or forty paces away I observed that the girl was leaning out, so I stopped and gave her a smile and a dignified bow. She returned my greeting, although just slightly, and then quickly withdrew. What a pretty girl she was! When I reached the end of the street I felt an overwhelming need to see her again, and I turned around, not without experiencing deep down a certain shame because neither my age nor my marital status warranted such improprieties—much less in the case of one so young. She was no longer on the balcony.

"Well, I thought to myself, I'm not leaving without seeing her, and I started to walk slowly up and down the street with the same cheek as a junior military officer—not taking my eyes off the house. After all, nobody here knows me, I kept thinking in order to have the courage to continue my walking. Besides, I didn't have anything to do then, and it made no difference if I idled away the time there or somewhere else.

"Just as I was crossing in front of the balcony for the third or fourth time, the charming creature appeared on it. On seeing me, she gave a start, made an adorable face, then broke out laughing and disappeared again.

"But how foolish and naive we men are when it comes to these matters! Would you believe that at the time I didn't even suspect that the girl had been watching my every move, not missing a single one!

"After I had satisfied my whim, I left Infantas Street and went to a friend's house. But the following day, whether by coincidence or design, more than likely the latter, I managed to pass by the same spot at the same time. My charming assailant, who was leaning over the balustrade looking down, turned red from ear to ear as soon as she recognized me and withdrew before I passed in front of the house. As you can imagine, this, far from disheartening me, encouraged me to anchor myself on the corner of the first intersection, in ecstatic contemplation. Four minutes hadn't elapsed when I saw the appearance of a pearly little nose, which swiftly withdrew, appeared again two minutes later and withdrew again, appeared again one minute later and withdrew once more. When she tired of such moves, she leaned all the way out and stared at me for some time, as if trying to demonstrate that she was not in the least afraid of me. Both of us then escalated a running fire of looks, accompanied, for my part, by all manner of smiles, waves, and assorted lethal projectiles which must have caused the enemy significant damage. A half hour later, the latter heard, undoubtedly in the living room, the "cease-fire" bugle call and withdrew, closing the balcony door.

"I won't have to tell you that, for as ashamed as I was of my little escapade, I continued to walk her street at the same hour and that our exchange of looks became more and more intense and lively. Three or four days later I decided to take a piece of paper from my wallet and write the following: *I like you very much.* I wrapped the paper around a coin to weight it and, taking advantage of a moment when nobody was in the area and after signaling to her to stand aside, I threw my message up to the balcony. The next day, as I was passing by, I saw a paper pellet fall, which I speedily retrieved and unfolded. It said, in large, slanted script, laboriously written, and on ruled paper to keep the words straight: *I like you two don't think I play with dolls it was my sister's.*

"Although I smiled as I read the billet-doux, it did not fail to produce a sweet, agreeable sensation in me, which very quickly gave way to another—a melancholy one, on remembering that such adventures were forever forbidden to me. That day my pretty correspondent didn't appear on the balcony, undoubtedly ashamed of her acquiescence, but the following day I found her ready and willing to engage in another round of looks, signs, and smiles, which both parties now used liberally. This game would last an hour or longer every afternoon, until she was called and hurriedly went inside. I asked her by means of signs if she went out for walks and she signaled that she did; and, in fact, one day I waited in the street until four o'clock and I saw her come out accompanied by a woman, who must have been her mother, and two younger brothers. I followed them to the Retiro, although at a respectable distance, because I would have been mortified if her mother had realized what was going on. The girl, exercising less prudence, turned around continually and smiled at me, which kept me in a constant state of alarm. In the end, we returned to the house without mishap. During all this time I didn't know what her name was, and in order to find out I wrote the question on another piece of paper from my wallet: *What's your name?* She answered in the same large, slanted script on the ruled paper: *My name is Teresa for heaven's sake don't think I play with dolls.*

"Almost two weeks went by in this way. Teresa seemed prettier to me by the day, and really was, because, as I've learned in the course of a lifetime, there is no painting, no piece of satin, nor any strip of brocade that makes a woman radiant with beauty like love. I asked her over and over again if we could talk, and she always responded that it was absolutely out of the question, because if her mother found out, that would be the end of the balcony! I began to suspect that I was falling in love and this made me uneasy. I couldn't think about that girl without experi-

encing a profound melancholy, as if she embodied my youth, my
golden dreams, all my hopes, which were forever separated from
me by an unsurmountable barrier. At the same time I was suffering pangs of remorse. Imagine my poor wife's grief if she ever
discovered that her husband was in the capital courting young
girls! One day I received a letter from her telling me that our
younger son was slightly ill and pleading with me to conclude
my business and return home at once. You can imagine how this
news upset me because my children have always been the apple
of my eye. And as if that were a providential punishment, or at
least a salutary warning, and after serious and lengthy medita-
tion, in which I reproached myself mercilessly for my detestable,
ludicrous conduct, I openly acknowledged the error of my ways
and resolved to abide immediately by my wife's request. In order
to carry through on this determination the first thing that occurred to me was not to think any more about Teresa, nor even
to walk along her street, although I couldn't avoid doing so, and
then to cut short my stay as much as possible. According to my
calculations, I would be free in five or six days.

"So I stopped strolling along Infantas Street, as had been my
custom after lunch—not even to reach Valverde Street, where
friends of mine lived. But after supper, at night, since there was
no danger of seeing Teresa, I would cross it rapidly and without
looking at her house.

"Four days went by. I no longer thought about her, or if I did,
it was in a vague way, like thinking about the happy days of
youth. I had almost wrapped up my business and was preoccupied with the selection of a departure date. At the latest, it'll be
Friday or Saturday, I said to myself as I lit a cigar and headed
outside after supper one night. The minister had refused to lower
Valencia's tax, which upset me a great deal. Mulling over what I
needed to recount to my colleagues upon my return and the best
way to explain the reason for my failure, I crossed Plaza del Rey
and turned onto Infantas Street. It was a mild, magnificent night,
and I wore my topcoat unbuttoned; I was walking slowly and
taking sensual delight in the temperature, the cigar, and the certainty of seeing my family soon. As I was passing in front of
Teresa's house, I stopped and looked at it for a moment, almost
with indifference. And I continued on my way, muttering: 'What
a cute girl! It'll be a shame if some good-for-nothing wins her!'

Afterwards I began to reflect on how easy it would have been for me to play a dirty trick on the mayor of Valencia and take his job away from him—but no, that would have been a betrayal. Even though he was somewhat headstrong and haughty, he was after all a friend. I still had time to be mayor.

"When I was most engrossed in my thoughts and political plans, and when I was just about to turn the corner of the street, an arm slipped through mine and a voice said to me:

"'Are you going far?'"

"'Teresa!'

"Both of us were silent for a few moments—I, gazing at her, thunderstruck, and she, with bowed head, holding on to my arm.

"'Where are you going at this hour of night?'"

"'I'm going with you,' she replied, raising her head and smiling as if she had said the most natural thing in the world.

"'Where?'"

"'How do I know? Wherever you want.'

"I felt shivers of pleasure and fear at the same time.

"'Have you run away from home?'"

"'Of course not! But I have pulled a fast one on Manuel! It's funny, you'll see what I mean. I insisted on wanting to go to my cousins' get-together today. They live on Fuencarral Street and Papa ordered Manuel to accompany me there. We arrived at the doorway where I told him to leave because I didn't need him any more. I pretended to climb the stairs, but turned around right away, without ringing, and then followed him back to the house. When I saw him go in I laughed so loud that he almost heard me.'

"She was still laughing, so freely and openly that I couldn't help but do the same.

"'And why did you do that?' I asked, with the lack of tact, or rather, with the brutishness that we gentlemen usually possess in abundance.

"'For no reason,' she replied, suddenly letting go of my arm and breaking into a run.

"I followed and quickly caught up with her.

"'Aren't you the touchy one!' I said, making a joke of it. 'What a way to say goodbye! Forgive me if I've offended you . . .'

"The girl, without saying a word, took my arm again. We walked for a good while in silence. I was thinking anxiously about what I was going to say and about what I was going to do. In the end, Teresa broke that silence, asking me resolutely:

"'Didn't you tell me in a letter that you loved me?'"

"'Well, of course I love you!'"

"'Then why have you stopped coming to see me and walking along the street during the day?'"

"'Because I was afraid that your mother . . .'"

"'Sure. It's because all you men are nothing but ingrates, and the more you're loved, the worse it becomes. You think I don't know? I've been out on the balcony every afternoon waiting for you . . . but what did you expect? At night, behind the windows, I saw you go by, very serious—very serious, without even looking toward my house. I would say to myself: I wonder if he's angry with me. But why would he be angry? Because I've closed the balcony at a quarter to three? In short, all I did was wonder and wonder, without making sense of it. Then I said to myself: I'm going to give him a scare tonight.'"

"'It's been a most agreeable scare.'"

"'If you hadn't stopped in front of my house and stood there looking at the balconies, I wouldn't have come out of the doorway; but that decided it for me.'

"There was a momentary silence during which I entertained a rush of thoughts that still embarrass me. Teresa stared at me again.

"'Are you pleased?'"

"'Naturally!'"

"'You're happy in my company?'"

"'More than with anyone else in the world.'"

"'I'm not bothering you?'"

"'On the contrary, I'm experiencing a pleasure that you can't imagine.'"

"'You have nothing to do now?'"

"'Absolutely nothing.'"

"'Then let's go for a walk. When the time comes, you'll take me home and Mama will assume that my cousins' servant brought me. But if I'm bothering you or you don't like walking with me, tell me . . . I'll go right now.'

"I answered by squeezing her arm and pulling gently on her hand to place it snugly inside mine. Teresa continued talking with amusing unpredictability.

"'It seems impossible that we're such good friends, doesn't it? I thought when I dropped the doll on your head that I had killed you. I was so afraid! If you could have seen . . . ! Tell me something: why did you smile instead of getting angry?'"

"'What a question! Because I took a liking to you.'"

"'That's what I thought—that you must have taken to me, because if not, the truth is that you had reason to be furious. When you brought it upstairs, I was still frightened to death, which is why I closed the door so fast. That no-good doll! It made me so angry that I threw it on the floor and broke one of its arms.'"

"'You shouldn't mistreat the poor thing; on the contrary, you ought to keep it as a remembrance.'"

"'You know something? You're right. If it hadn't been for the doll, we wouldn't have met . . . , nor would you be my boyfriend . . . , because I have another one . . .'"

"'What do you mean, another one?'"

"'I mean, I don't have one any more, but I used to. A cousin who's determined that I'm to love him against my will. Don't go thinking that he's ugly; quite the opposite, he's good-looking, but I don't like him. I can't help it. I said yes because I took pity on him one day when he started crying.'

"As we talked like this, we calmly walked the streets. To avoid any of the girl's relatives or acquaintances, I sought out the least frequented ones. Teresa had taken my arm as you would that of an old friend and was talking incessantly, and laughing; sometimes she would shake me vigorously and maybe stop in front of a shop window to have me look at some trinket. Her conversation was a sweet, suggestive birdsong that moved me and gladdened my heart. Because of it, the mass of perfidious thoughts that were roaming my mind began to disappear little by little. Without my knowing how, all my fears vanished too. I imagined that Teresa was somehow related to me, and I didn't consider our situation unusual and dangerous as I had in the beginning. Her innocence was a dense veil that prevented us from seeing the risk that we were running.

"In short order she told me a thousand different things. She was from Jerez de la Frontera; the family had been settled in Madrid only for a year; her father occupied an important position; and she had two younger brothers and one younger sister. She described in some detail their character and ways: the sister was a good little girl, pleasant and obedient, but the boys were insufferable, and all day long they shouted, dirtied the house, and fought. Her mother had given her authority over them, even to mete out punishment, something she resisted doing because she feared she would lose their affection—let her mother deal with them as best she could. Afterwards she talked about her father, who was a very serious but a very good man. The only thing that distressed her was that he seemed to love the boys more than their sisters. The mother, on the other hand, favored the girls. Then she told me about her cousins—the girls—who lived on Fuencarral Street. One was very pretty; the other, only amusing; both had a boyfriend, each of whom was useless—mere boys, high school students. Their brother was the male cousin who had been her boyfriend; he was already a high school graduate who was getting ready to enter the army's artillery school. From time to time, in the brief intervals of silence, she would gracefully raise her head and ask me:

"'You're happy in my company? I'm not bothering you?'

"And when she heard me protest sharply against such doubts, her expressive face would light up with joy and she would resume talking.

"We had walked a number of streets, and you can imagine that I was enjoying myself—like the angels in paradise. I was hanging on the words of that girl who, as she related to me all the cute things she had done as a child, seemed to instill in my enchanted spirit the knowledge of happiness. Nevertheless, I was unable to dispel a vague anxiety that detracted from my joy. As we were seeking a more dignified way of spending the time at our disposal than roaming the streets, we came upon the Royal Theater at the bottom of Santo Domingo. The idea of going in occurred to me instantly. Teresa accepted at once, and in order not to call attention to ourselves, we bought tickets to the top gallery. *I Puritani* was being performed and it was jammed with people, which made it difficult for us to squeeze through to go up to one of the corners, but we finally reached it. Teresa was pleased as Punch and repaid me for the trouble that I had gone through to get her there with endless smiles and kind words. While the curtain was being raised we continued to chat, although very softly. We had become rather familiar with each other and she let me take one of her hands, which I caressed, enraptured.

"When the opera began, she stopped talking and gave it her

undivided attention, so much so that the sight of her ecstatic eyes and cute little head leaning against the wall brought a smile to my lips. Although familiar with music, she had been to the theater so infrequently that the inspired melodies of Bellini's opera made a profound impression on her, which caused a slight twitch in her eyes and lips. When the time came for the tenor's sublime aria, which begins 'A te, o cara,' she squeezed my hand, whispering, 'Oh, how beautiful, how beautiful!' Afterwards she had me explain to her what was happening on the stage. She thought the tenor and soprano's upcoming marriage most fitting, but truly pitied the baritone, whose fiancée was being stolen from him; she became highly upset at the end of the second act when the tenor is obliged to accompany the queen and forsake his intended, and stated in no uncertain terms that she found such conduct contemptible.

"'But bear in mind that he was compelled to do so because it was his queen who was asking.'"*

"'That doesn't matter, that doesn't matter. If he really loved her, no queen could force him. The fiancée always comes first.'

"It was impossible for me to drive that strange theory from her mind. After the curtain came down, we stayed in our seats and she insisted that I tell her my life story: how many girlfriends I had had, which one I had loved most, etc., etc. You'll understand that I needed to string together one lie after another. Then, for no good reason, she declared that all men were ungrateful. I dared to point out that there were exceptions, but she would have none of it.

"'You'll be just like all the others (she announced in a prophetic tone, staring at a point in space); you'll love me for a little while, and then you'll forget all about me.'

"What a delightful and simultaneously maddening time that girl was putting me through! To steer the conversation in another direction, I asked her:

"'How old are you? As yet you haven't told me.'"

"'I'm . . . I'm . . . Look, I always say that I'm fourteen, but the truth is that I'm just a little over thirteen, by two months . . . And you?'"

"'It's shocking! Don't ask because it embarrasses me.'"

"'Ah, how vain! Why, I'll love you whether you're old or young!'

"Right away she proposed that we use the familiar form of

address. But after I accepted she backed down, suggested that I use it with her while she would continue to use the formal form with me. I refused to go along.

"'Well, look, I can't use the familiar with you—it would embarrass me too much . . . But, all right, let's try.'

"We learned from the trial run that, to avoid the pronoun, the poor thing continually beat around the bush and enmeshed herself in an endless series of circumlocutions. If she ventured to use a familiar you, she would do so in a lowered voice and ill at ease.

"When the second act began, she turned her attention again to the stage. I almost never stopped looking at her face, while she, with her eyes half-closed, smiled at me frequently, squeezing my hand at the same time. I noticed, nevertheless, that her bright countenance had dimmed a little, and that she was losing the amusing unpredictability that I observed earlier. The smiles on her lips were becoming sad, and a streak of worry clouded her innocent brow, lending her pretty face an unnaturally serious expression. It appeared that by virtue of a mysterious shift in her spirit the girl was rapidly being transformed into a woman. She stopped squeezing my hand and even withdrew hers. I furtively took it back into mine, but a short time later she withdrew it once more.

"The second act had ended. As the curtain was being lowered, she had me take out my watch, and seeing that it was eleven o'clock, said that we needed to leave immediately because at eleven-thirty—at the very latest—the servant was coming after her.

"On exiting the theater we found it necessary to avoid going near the carriages that were lined up at the entrance. It was still a mild, starry night. In the streets there was no longer the bustle of the early hours, but even so we chose the most solitary route. Teresa refused to take my arm as she had before.

"Then it fell to me to be expansive, and I whispered in her ear a thousand compliments and sweet nothings, explaining in detail the love that she had awakened in me and how I had suffered on the days when I didn't pass along her street. I recounted to her all the particulars—even the most insignificant ones—of our brand of sign language and our correspondence; and I described the clothes that I had seen her wear, as well as the finery, to get her to understand the profound impression she had made on me. My outpouring elicited no response, Teresa just kept walking in a downcast, worried manner which contrasted sharply with her demeanor as we passed by the same places three hours earlier. When I paused for a moment to draw my breath, she exclaimed while averting her eyes:

"'I've done something very bad, very bad. Good Lord, if Papa found out!'

"I tried to convince her that her father couldn't find out about anything because we would get back too early.

"'In any event, even if Papa doesn't find out, I've done something very bad. You know it too, but you don't want to admit it. Isn't it true that a well-bred girl wouldn't do what I've done tonight? If my cousins found out . . . the two who are always hoping to catch me doing something wrong! But don't you go thinking . . . for heaven's sake . . . that I've done it with evil intentions. I'm very impetuous. Everybody says so. But everybody also says that I'm a good person at heart.'

"As she was saying this, Teresa got such a lump in her throat that she started weeping uncontrollably. I had a very hard time calming her down, but finally succeeded by praising her open, unaffected character and good-heartedness and promising that I would always love and respect her. She made me swear a dozen times that I didn't think ill of her and, after drying her tears, regained her sunny disposition and began to talk nonstop. In short order she proposed a thousand different schemes, each one more absurd than the other. One suggestion was that I go to her house the next day and ask her father for her hand. The father would say that his daughter was too young, but I was to respond at once that age didn't matter at all; the father would then insist that it was much too soon, and I would cite the precedent set by his own aunt, his mother's sister, who was playing with dolls when she was told to ready herself to be married. What could he adduce to oppose this powerful argument? Nothing, for sure. We'd get married and immediately afterwards journey to Jerez for me to meet her friends and aunt and uncle. What a scare it would give them all to see her on the arm of a gentleman, and even more so when they learned that this gentleman was her husband!

"She looked so pretty and alluring that I couldn't help making a passionate request that she allow me to give her a kiss. She refused. No man had yet kissed her. Only her cousin had stolen one, but he paid for it dearly because she spilled two glasses of lemonade over his head, and even in games like blindman's buff she insisted on outstretched hands so that nobody's lips would touch her face. But when we were married, it would be another matter; then I could give her all the kisses I had a mind to, although she suspected that I wouldn't ask with as much ardor as now.

"We were nearing her house. The carriages of people who were returning from evening visits drowned Teresa out as they rolled by us, forcing her to raise her voice a little. From the sky, the stars winked at us as if issuing an invitation to hurry in our enjoyment of those happy moments which would never return. In the distance only nightwatchmen's lamps, twinkling like ignes fatui, could be seen.

"We finally arrived. In front of the door Teresa made me swear again that I harbored no uncharitable thoughts about her, and that the following afternoon, at two on the dot, I would appear under her balcony.

"'Be sure to come.'"

"'I'll come, beautiful.'"

"'At two on the dot?'"

"'At two on the dot.'"

"'Now knock on the door.'

"I knocked loudly on the door. Shortly we heard the doorman approaching.

"'Now,' she said in a low, shaky voice, 'give me a kiss and leave quickly.'

"She then offered me her rosy, innocent cheek. I took it in my hands and planted a kiss on it . . . then two . . . three . . . , four . . . . , as many as I could until I heard the key turn in the lock. And then I hurried away."

Don Ramón stopped talking.

"And what happened afterwards?" I asked with keen interest.

"Nothing. That night I couldn't sleep from remorse and the next day I took the train home."

"Without seeing Teresa?"

"Without seeing Teresa."

Notes

Page references to this volume precede each note.

(19)   *Arbín:* all the place names and rivers in this story are real and located in Asturias and the northern part of (what today is called) Castilla y León.

(25)   *Polyphemus:* a Cyclops (giants with a single round eye in the middle of the forehead) whom Odysseus and his men blinded to escape imprisonment.

(34)   *jotas . . . sevillanas:* popular Spanish dances (of Aragon and Andalusia).

(34)   *Our . . . Carmel:* Mt. Carmel, in what today is NW Israel, where— tradition has it—the first chapel was built in honor of the Blessed Virgin.

(35)   *La Favorita:* opera (1840) by Gaetano Donizetti (1797–1848).

(35)   *peteneras . . . . malagueñas:* popular Andalusian songs.

(35)   *L'Africaine:* opera (1865) by Giacomo Meyerbeer (1791–1864).

(44)   *Máiquez . . . Luna:* Isidoro Máiquez (1768–1820), considered the best Spanish actor of his time; Rita Luna (1770–1832), considered the best Spanish actress of her time.

(49)   *Calderón:* Pedro Calderón de la Barca, one of the truly outstanding figures in Spanish literary history, a Golden Age playwright whose best-known play is *Life is a Dream.*

(56)   *Espoz . . . Street:* in Madrid.

(58)   *Tata:* a term used by children to refer to their nursemaid.

(59)   *Gayarre:* Julián Gayarre (1843–90), Spanish tenor; judged one of the greatest opera singers of all times.

(59)   *Chucho:* a diminutive, along with *Chunchín* (p. 65), of Jesús.

(64)   *Chipilín:* affectionate term to refer to a child.

(69)   *Etchings:* Palacio Valdés is referring to a book [*Aguasfuertes*], published in 1884, made up of both articles and short stories. Three of the latter included here are: *The Bird in the Snow, Drama in the Flies,* and *Clotilde's Romance.*

(74)   *Escrich:* Enrique Pérez Escrich (1829–97), serial novelist popular during the nineteenth century; completely ignored today.

(74)   *Sanz del Río:* Julián Sanz del Río (1814–69), Spanish educator and proponent of the doctrines of the German philosopher Christian Friedrich Krause (1781–1832).

(82)   *Ayala:* Adelardo López de Ayala (1828–79), playwright who contributed to establishing the realist mode in the theater; best known for *Consuelo* (1878).

(84)   *Núñez . . . Grilo:* Gaspar Núñez de Arce (1834–1903), poet and playwright; Antonio Fernández Grilo (1845–1906), immensely popular poet during his lifetime, almost completely ignored today.

(84)   *Tamayo:* Manuel Tamayo y Baus (1829–98); along with López de Ayala

133

he contributed to the transition from Romanticism to Realism; his best play is *A New Drama* (1867), cited on p. 86.

(86) *Gutiérrez:* Antonio García Gutiérrez (1813–84), playwright best known for two Romantic works, *The Troubadour* (1836) and *Simón Bocanegra* (1843), the basis of two of Verdi's operas.

(87) *high life:* in English in the original.

(101) *Atocha:* One of the many designations of the Blessed Virgin in Spain. According to tradition, an apostle from Antioch brought a statue of her to the outskirts of Madrid where he erected a hermitage in an esparto field which in Spanish is *atochal*, hence our Lady of Atocha; numerous miracles were attributed to her holy image.

(107) *louis:* louis d'or, gold coins (formerly) used in France.

(109) *Büchner's . . . Matter:* Friedrich Karl Christian Ludwig Büchner (1824–99), German philosopher and physician whose greatest work was *Kraft und Stoff* [*Force and Matter*] (1855), in which he attempted to demonstrate the indestructibility of matter and force, elements that he viewed as infinite.

(118) *I Puritani* (1835): by the Italian opera composer Vincenzo Bellini (1801–35).

(119) The libretto reads:

Bel sogno beato	(Beautiful, blissful dream
Di pace e contento	Of peace and contentment)
. . . .	
La dolce memoria	(The sweet memory
D'un tenero amore	Of a tender love)

Vincenzo Bellini, *I Puritani.* Libretto, Carlo Pepoli; Eng. trans. William Weaver (New York: G. Schirmer, 1975), p. 2.

(129) Don Ramón's view is somewhat at variance with the libretto. Arturo *offers* to escort the queen to safety, she does not ask that he do so; on the contrary, she implores Arturo to desist and think of Elvira, who awaits him "at the holy altar."

Original Titles

El potro del señor cura/The Curate's Colt

Polifemo/Polyphemus

El pájaro en la nieve/The Bird in the Snow

El drama de las bambalinas/Drama in the Flies

El crimen de la calle de la Perseguida/The Crime on
  Perseguida Street

¡Solo!/Alone!

Seducción/Seduction

Los amores de Clotilde/Clotilde's Romance

Merci, Monsieur/_____

Las burbujas/Bubbles

Sociedad primitiva/Primitive Society

Un testigo de cargo/A Witness for the Prosecution

Perico el Bueno/Perico the Good

Vida de canónigo/The Life of a Canon

Los Puritanos/I Puritani

Select Bibliography

English Translations of Palacio Valdés's Novels

The Marquis of Peñalta [*Marta y María*]. Trans. Nathan Haskell Dole. New York: Crowell, 1886.

Maximina [*Maximina*]. Trans. Nathan Haskell Dole. New York and Boston: Crowell, 1888.

Sister Saint Sulpice [*La hermana San Sulpicio*]. Trans. Nathan Haskell Dole. New York: Crowell, 1890, 1925.

Scum [*La espuma*]. Anon. trans. New York: United States Book Co., 1890.

Froth [*La espuma*]. Trans. Clara Bell. London: Heinemann, 1891. (New York: U.S. Book, 1891.)

Faith [*La fe*]. Trans. Isabel F. Hapgood. New York: Cassell, 1892.

The Grandee [*El maestrante*]. Trans. Rachel Challice. London: Heinemann, 1894. (New York: Peck, 1895.)

The Origin of Thought [*El origen del pensamientol*]. Trans. Isabel F. Hapgood. Abridgment in *Cosmopolitan* magazine (New York), 16 (1893) pp. 436–58, 542–57, 706–26; 17 (1894), pp. 86–101, 185–202, 335–51, 485–94.

The Joy of Captain Ribot [*La alegría del capitán Ribot*]. Trans. Minna Caroline Smith. London: Downey, 1900. (New York: Brentano's, 1922. London: World Fiction Library, 1923.)

The Fourth Estate [*El cuarto poder*]. Trans. Rachel Challice. New York: Brentano's; London: Richards, 1901.

José [*José*]. Trans. Minna Caroline Smith. New York: Brentano's, 1901. (New York: Translation, 1931.)

José [*José*]. Trans. Harriet de Onís. Great Neck, NY: Barron's 1961.

Tristán [*Tristán o el pesimismo*]. Trans. Jane B. Reid. Boston: Four Seas, 1925.

English Translations of Palacio Valdés's Short Stories

"Bird in the Snow" ["El pájaro en la nieve"]. In *Christmas Stories from French and Spanish Writers*. Trans. Antoinette Ogden. Chicago: McClurg, 1892.

"The Loves of Clotilde" ["Los amores de Clotilde"]. In *Tales from the Italian and Spanish*. Anon. trans. New York: Review of Reviews, 1920.

"The Crime in the Street of the Persecution" ["El crimen de la calle de la Perseguida"]. In *Tales from the Italian and Spanish*. Anon. trans. New York: Review of Reviews, 1920.

"Polyphemus" ["Polifemo"]. In *Tales from the Italian and Spanish*. Anon. trans. New York: Review of Reviews, 1920.

"I Puritani" ["Los puritanos"]. In *Poet Lore*. 1905; 16: 97–108. Trans. S. G. Morley.

Original Spanish Texts of Palacio Valdés's Works

There are two accessible Spanish editions of Palacio Valdés's writings: the *Obras completas* published by Ediciones Fax (Madrid) from the mid 1940s to the late 1950s in thirty-one (31) volumes and the *Obras* published by Aguilar (Madrid) in 1959 in two (2) volumes. Both editions contain all the novels, short stories, literary criticism, autobiography, and miscellany. The Fax edition, however, is not in any sense "complete." It was just a few years ago, for example, that Brian J. Dendle published in the *Boletín del Instituto de Estudios Asturianos* articles that Palacio Valdés had written for the Madrid newspaper *ABC* in the 1930s.

"The Curate's Colt"/"Polyphemus"/"The Bird in the Snow"/"Drama in the Flies"/"The Crime on Perseguida Street"/"Clotilde's Romance" and "I Puritani" are in Fax IV *(Aguas fuertes)* and Aguilar II *(Obras)*.

"Primitive Society"/"A Witness for the Prosecution"/"Bubbles"/"Perico the Good"/"Merci, Monsieur" and "The Life of a Canon" are in Fax XIX *(Papeles del doctor Angélico)* and Aguilar I *(Obras*.

"Seduction" and "Alone!" are in Fax XXII *(Seducción y otros cuentos)* and Aguilar II *(Obras)*.

A recent collection of short stories is: *El pájaro en la nieve y otros cuentos* [*The Bird in the Snow and Other Stories*]. Ed. Carmen Bravo-Villasante. Madrid: Mondadori, 1990. It contains: *"El pájaro en la nieve"* ["The Bird in the Snow"], "La confesión de un crimen" ["Confessing a Crime"], "El crimen de la calle de la Perseguida" ["The Crime on Perseguida Street"], "El potro del señor cura" ["The Curate's Colt"], "Polifemo" ["Polyphemus"], "Los Puritanos" ["I Puritani"], "El cachorrillo" ["The Pistol"], and "Caballería infantil" ["Childhood Battles"].

Secondary Sources in English

Bly, Peter A. "*La fe:* Palacio Valdés Looks Back to Alas and Forward to Unamuno." *Romance Quarterly*. 1988 Aug.; 35 (3): 339–346.

Capellán Gonzalo, Angel. "William Dean Howells and Armando Palacio Valdés." *Revista de Estudios Hispánicos*. 1976; 10: 451–471.

Charnon-Deutsch, Lou. *The Nineteenth Century Spanish Story: Textual Strategies of a Genre in Transition*. London: Tamesis, 1985.

Childers, J. Wesley. "Sources of Palacio Valdés' *Las burbujas*." *Hispania*. 1958; 41: 181–185.

Dendle, Brian J. "The Early Writings of Armando Palacio Valdés." 55–61 in Martín, Gregorio C., ed. *Selected Proceedings of the Pennsylvania Foreign Language Conference*. Pittsburgh: Duquesne Univ., Dept. of Mod. Langs.; 1988. 192 pp.

O'Connor, D.J. "Mrs. Humphry Ward's *Robert Elsmere* (1888) and Palacio Valdés's *La fe* (1892)." *Romance Quarterly*. 1990 Aug.; 37(3): 331–336.

———. "Flirtation, the Eucharist and the Grotesque in Palacio Valdés' *La fe* (1892)." *Letras Peninsulares*. 1988 Spring; 1(1): 51–69.

Ullman, Pierre L. "José as a Male Cinderella." *Romance Quarterly*. 1988 Aug.; 35(3): 331–337.

Valis, Noël M. "Palacio Valdés' First Novel." *Romance Notes*. 1980; 20: 317–321.

Wells, Lila Charlotte. "Palacio Valdés' Vision of Women in His Novels and Essays." *Dissertation Abstracts International*. 1981 July; 42(1): 242A–243A.

Wood, Jennifer Jenkins. "Religious Themes in the Novels of Armando Palacio Valdés." *Dissertation Abstracts International*. 1982 July; 43(1): 179A.

———. "Armando Palacio Valdés's *La fe*: Providential Novel." *Hispanic Journal*. 1985 Fall; 7(1): 51–57.

Secondary Sources in Spanish and Italian

Ateneo Jovellanos (Centro asturiano de Buenos Aires). Buenos Aires, 1953 (Palacio Valdés: Homenaje en el primer centenario de su nacimiento, 1853 octubre 1953).

Baquero Goyanes, Mariano. *El cuento español en el siglo XIX*. Madrid: C.S.I.C., 1949.

Boletín del Instituto de Estudios Asturianos. Oviedo, 1953; 7(19) [Issue of articles about Palacio Valdés on the centenary of his birth].

Caudet, Francisco. "Armando Palacio Valdés: Alcance ideológico de *La aldea perdida*." *Diálogos Hispánicos de Amsterdam*. 1984; 4: 109–123.

Cruz Rueda, Angel. *Armando Palacio Valdés. Su vida y su obra*. 2nd ed. Madrid: Saeta, 1949.

Dendle, Brian J. "Las variantes textuales de *El señorito Octavio*, de Armando Palacio Valdés." *Boletín del Instituto de Estudios Asturianos*. 1987; 41: 463–474.

———. "'Covadonga, tres etapas': Un artículo no recogido de Armando Palacio Valdés." *Boletín del Instituto de Estudios Asturianos*. 1988: 42(128): 831–835.

———. "Erotismo y anticlericalismo en la primera edición de *Marta y María*, de Armando Palacio Valdés." *Boletín de la Biblioteca de Menéndez Pelayo*. 1989; 65: 305–316.

———. "Los artículos de Armando Palacio Valdés en ABC, 1932–1936." *Boletín del Instituto de Estudios Asturianos*. 1990; 44: 233–279.

Escobedo, Armando J. "Proyección literaria del carlismo religioso en la novelística española." *Diálogos Hispánicos de Amsterdam*. 1984; 4: 109–123. [*Marta y María*]

Fernández Alvarez, Jesús. "Un probable eco de Henry Fielding en *Le fe* de Armando Palacio Valdés." *Filología Moderna*. 1969; 33–34: 101–108.

García Blanco, Manuel. "El novelista asturiano Palacio Valdés y Unamuno." *Archivum*. 1958; 8: 5–13.

Gómez-Ferrer, Guadalupe. *Palacio Valdés y el mundo social de la Restauración*. Oviedo: Instituto de Estudios Asturianos, 1983.

González Fernández, José. "Aspectos regionales en Jovellanos, Palacio Valdés y Clarín." *Boletín del Instituto de Estudios Asturianos*. 1987; 41: 433–461.

Paolini, Gilbert. "La psicopatología en la literatura italo-española: D'Annunzio y Palacio Valdés." 275–289 en Bugliani, Americo, ed. *The Two Hesperias: Literary Studies in Honor of Joseph G. Fucilla on the Occasion of His 80th Birthday*. Madrid: Porrúa; 1977. 369 pp.

————. "Amalia: un caso patológico en *El Maestrante*." *Boletín de la Biblioteca de Menéndez Pelayo*. 1988 Jan.–Dec.; 64: 253–261.

————. "Palacio Valdés y el naturalismo ideal en *La alegría del capitán Ribot*." *Letras Peninsulares*. 1989 spring; 2(1): 19–29.

————. "Resonancia armónica del mundo mágico, creadora del porvenir regeneracional en *La alegría del capitán Ribot*." 479–485 en Fernández Jiménez, Juan et al, eds. *Estudios en homenaje a Enrique Ruiz Fornells*. Erie: Asociación de Licenciados y Doctores Españoles en Estados Unidos; 1990. 706 pp.

Pascual Rodríguez, Manuel. *Palacio Valdés. Teoría y práctica novelística*. Madrid: S.G.E.L., 1976.

Pitollet, Camille. "Recuerdos de don Armando Palacio Valdés." *Boletín de la Biblioteca de Menéndez Pelayo*. 1957; 33: 72–120.

Roca Franquesa, José María. *Palacio Valdés: técnica novelística y credo estético*. Oviedo: Instituto de Estudios Asturianos, 1951.

————. "Clases sociales y tipos representativos en la novelística de Armando Palacio Valdés: discurso leído por el autor en el acto de su solemne recepción académica el día 13 de marzo de 1980." Discurso de ingreso en la Real Academia Española.

Romano Colangeli, Maria. *Armando Palacio Valdés, Romanziere*. Lecce: Ed. Milella, 1957.

Sánchez Escribano, Federico. "*Lolita* de Nabokov y *Los Puritanos* de Palacio Valdés (Un paralelismo literario)." Vol. 2, 153–156 en *Homenaje a Rodríguez Moñino*. Madrid: Castalia, 1966.